ACKNOWLEDGMENTS

Putting my novel in the hands of friends and asking for their thoughts is like handing them my heart, asking them to slice it open, and carefully examine the contents. They aren't just holding a story I've written, they're holding a piece of me; a piece that could easily be misunderstood or, worse yet, allow them to see me more clearly. I find myself puttering around the house, more than slightly distracted, anxiously awaiting word that the last page has been turned. The waiting is almost as laborious as the writing itself; if I'm being honest.

With that being said, it is with the deepest gratitude that I thank my friends (and family) who gave their time, their honest feedback, and constructive criticism, all the while handling my heart with care. To Monica Monachino, Marva Baus, JoAnn Franks, Amelia Parks, and Chelsea Andres, THANK YOU! You each contributed thoughts and ideas that made this story even better than I imagined. The waiting was worth it.

Thank you to my editor, Mackenzie Conway. You shaped the Moore family in a way I couldn't have done on my own. I appreciate you more than you know.

Thank you, Lydia Schreiber, for your beautiful artwork. I love knowing my cover art is one of a kind. What a blessing to have such talented friends!

Thank you, Alison Sties of Sties Designs, for working your creative magic!

And to my husband, Chad: thank you for loving me, supporting me, and encouraging me to write. Thank you for seeing me more clearly than anyone and for not running away. Xoxo

Beth Ann Baus

My So Much More

A novel

by

Beth Ann Baus

Beth Ann Baus

ISBN: 9781654684266

1

Monday

My brother always said they'd write a book about his life. I always knew he was right. But what I didn't know was that "they" would be me. I would write a book about his life. I would tell the tale.

I've spent the last hour staring at my computer screen. My fingers have become numb from hovering over the keys. It's as if I have no fingers, and soon the numbness will travel up to my wrists, and it will be as if I have no hands, which wouldn't be the worst thing, really, not having hands. Perhaps then I could go to my publisher and, rather than beg for pardon, hold up my nubs and say, "It can't be done." But, apparently, there's technology now that will type the words for me as I speak them. I hate technology.

My husband Wes doesn't understand why I won't just tell them the truth. "Be honest," he says, "tell them it was insensitive to ask."

"I've been through enough," I should say. "He's only been dead three months. It's too soon. I shouldn't be asked to relive this horrific part of my life."

"But who better to tell the story?" they'll ask. "You were there," they'll say. "Who else could tell the tale?" They'll have a point.

Of course, what Wes wants to say is, "Just tell them 'no' like a normal person. Normal people don't wish their hands away in order to get out of writing a book." But he doesn't say this because he's heard my honest response a million times. He knows my words by heart: "Being normal is hard for me."

BE HONEST. I imagined the words appearing letter by letter on the screen. Do these words even mean anything anymore? The words sit ghostlike before my eyes, slightly blurred. The problem with being honest is that the truth can be just as damaging as a lie. I can write a story that resembles my brother's life, but then I must live with myself for not being honest, for painting the portrait of one man while using colors and textures that weren't his own. The other option is to tell the whole truth. Paint an accurate portrait. But, there are consequences at the end of that road as well. Telling his whole story, his true story, means also telling mine. Our stories are intertwined and inseparable. Our story also includes my daughter; her story is another link in the chain that binds us together, and I'm not ready to share that part of her, to paint that picture, if I'm being honest.

"Mom, you're being torpid."

"What?" I blinked until Finn's face became clear. He stood at the door holding an oversized Batman action figure, a gift from his grandfather.

"You're being torpid," he said again, brushing the thick curls from his eyes. He desperately needed a haircut. "It means—"

"I know what torpid means," I interrupted, clearing my throat. "And I'm not torpid. I'm thinking."

"You think slow."

"I don't think slow. I think deep."

"I'm gonna be late for school." He walked away, half rolling his eyes as to only be half disrespectful.

I typed the sentence, "How many nine-year-olds know the word *torpid*?" Apparently, my fingers still worked after all.

In the kitchen, my hands proved their worth by making breakfast, packing lunches, and untangling Finn's shoestrings, and then again by inserting the car key into the ignition. I watched in wonder as my fingers gripped the gear stick, thrusting us into reverse and then sending us on our way. Hands, I decided, were all too often overlooked and underappreciated. I would be thankful not to have nubs and find a different excuse for not writing the book.

"You have a test today?" I asked Sadie on the drive to school.

"Biology," she mumbled.

"Are you prepared?"

"I studied if that's what you're asking." She leaned back against the headrest.

"You look pale."

"Thanks a lot." She rolled her eyes and turned her face away from me.

"You're holding your stomach. Does it hurt?"

She quickly moved her hands and rubbed them down her thighs. She looked at me and mouthed, "PMS" by overexaggerating the letters, as if my eyesight were failing.

"Oh, okay." I raised my eyebrows and shrugged my shoulders. She went back to staring out the window.

I reached to turn on the radio to find something we could sing together but then remembered we don't do that anymore. So I turned to look at Finn in the backseat. He was playing with Batman.

"Finn, honey. What happened to Batman's cape?"

He held Batman at eye level and examined the black material as I stopped the car in front of the high school.

"I cut it off. It was too long," Finn explained.

"See ya," Sadie said with absolutely no expression. "You don't need to pick me up after school. I'm going to Claire's to study. She'll bring me home later."

I wanted to say in a raised voice, "You're going to Claire's? You spent the entire weekend at her house." But, the voice inside whispered, "Pick your battles."

So, trying to sound equally nonchalant I said, "Sure, that's fine."

Sadie closed the door, a little too hard for my liking. I bit my bottom lip as I watched her walk away.

"Mom, I want to be punctual," Finn whined.

"Sorry." I completely rolled my eyes and then hoped he didn't see.

I drove across the lot past the high school to the elementary building and joined the never-ending line of minivans.

"Finn? Why did you cut Batman's cape?"

"I told you, it was too long."

"Are you sure you cut it?"

"What do you mean?"

"Well, one time when I was about your age my mom asked me why my doll's hair was all cut off. I told her that I had cut it, but really . . ."

"Really what?"

I inched forward in the line of traffic. I let my window down, just enough to feel the breeze. Or, maybe it was to let the images in my head escape.

"Really what?" Finn asked again.

"Nothing. You can get out now."

"Tell Grandma I said hi. And tell her she has the best forgetter of anyone I know."

"I'm not going to tell her that."

"I know. That's a private 'just-between-us' remark, not a public 'to-her-face' remark." He smiled and tossed Batman in the seat; his plastic head thumped against the seat belt buckle. "And, Mom, I know it's hard, but try to be normal today." Finn closed the door and, unlike his sister, turned to smile and wave at me before running to meet his classmates. I wouldn't mind Sadie being nine years old again. I also wouldn't mind going back in time and never verbalizing that being normal is hard for me.

As I inched towards the exit, anxious like the other parents to get on with my day, I found myself wondering about Wes, the kids, and this town. Wesley's ancestors had founded this small Ohio town, a prestige which has been held over the heads of children, including our own, for generations. "Your ancestors would roll over in their graves if they knew you did that," parents would say. "Don't disgrace your heritage" was a favorite of Wesley's grandfather.

When Wes graduated from the police academy, he patted his dad on the back and said he intended to spend his life defending this town and his heritage. Now I feared bringing shame, not only to our family but to the long line of Moore's. "Their blood didn't run through her veins," they would say about me. "She isn't really a Moore."

I glanced in the rearview mirror and tugged at my cheek, patches of my face were going numb, pins and needles. The car behind me honked its horn, something that only felt rude if you were the one being honked at. I raised my hand and slightly ducked my head, a strange sort of acknowledgment and half-hearted apology. I took a deep breath, shook my head, and tried not to cry—something I had every reason and also no particular reason to do.

I unlocked the front door to my mother-in-law's house and called her name several times before she answered—this always made my heart beat heavy.

"I'm in here. In my bedroom." The pep in her voice made me smile and offered great relief. I walked through the hallway lined with boxes and bare walls, except for one picture frame that had yet to come down. The cherry frame held a certificate that read, "Vernon Wesley Moore, Citizen of the Year." Stuck in the corner of the frame was a limp photograph of Wes holding his mother's arm as she accepted the award; Vernon had not lived long enough to attend the ceremony. I ran my fingers over his name as I walked by and imagined LuAnne leaving her home at the end of the week with this treasure tucked under her arm rather than packed in a box.

I found LuAnne sitting in a chair looking out the window, large pink rollers haphazardly hanging from her head.

"What are you looking at?" I asked.

"Hummingbirds on my feeder. They're just so sweet. Come slowly so you don't scare them away."

I tiptoed to her side and spoke softly, "I wonder if we could hear their wings if your window were open."

"They're going a mile a minute, aren't they? One last feast before the cold weather sets in." She took in a deep breath, held it for a moment, and then let it out slowly. She looked up at me with her silky brown eyes, "How's my favorite daughter-in-law today?"

"I'm not sure yet."

"Well, there's plenty of time to decide." Then pointing to her head, she asked, "Would you mind taking these out? They're starting to itch."

LuAnne sat like a statue, watching the tiny winged creatures flit and flutter; I stood behind her and gently removed the rollers one by one. Her hair was still thick and held a lovely mix of salt and pepper. She told me once that her hair was all the envy of the other ladies in her card club, then she tossed her hair back and let out a feminine laugh that could be mistaken for overconfidence, but it was something else entirely.

As she stared out the window, I began running my fingers through her hair, separating the large, unnatural curls. I was always pleased to do this job as the slow, repetitive motion relaxed me as much as it did her. I stood with my eyes closed, and as I felt her body relax, my mind began to wander: a habit I frequently indulged in. The dream world in my mind seemed more natural than the one I was born into, and transporting there had not only given me countless stories to put on paper but had also provided me an escape from the real world that never fully satisfied. There was, I admit, a particular danger in creating attachments in a world that didn't exist, reliving and perfecting moments that would never come to pass. But, there was also a comfort in knowing that place, that secret place, was only a thought away when the need for escape became too great.

My need for escape had been great for some time, perhaps for as long as I can remember. But, for the past three months, the grievances of my reality had managed to burrow into my wandering—leaving me apprehensive as I closed my eyes and traveled to my oasis, not sure of what light or darkness would meet me there. My fantasies had been hijacked by the very memories I traveled great distances to avoid, reminding me that, even with the best of working imaginations, there is no real escape.

On this day, as I closed my eyes, I found myself sitting on the floor of my childhood bedroom. My favorite doll squeezed between my knees; I was humming as I ran my fingers through her stiff, tangled hair. There was a knock at my door and thinking it was my mother, I absentmindedly said, "Come in."

It wasn't my mother. Instead, my brother stepped in and slowly closed the door.

"What do you want?" I asked, curling my toes.

"Nothing. I just wondered if you wanted to play."

"With you?"

"Yeah, with me? Who else? Are you playing with your doll? Can I see her?" He snatched her from my hands, and before I could react he pulled a pair of scissors from his back pocket and started cutting off her hair in thick, uneven chunks.

"What are you doing?" I screamed.

"Shut up!" he growled, gritting his teeth. "If you tell mom I did this, you'll be sorry."

"Give me my dolly," I whined.

He finished butchering her hair and threw her back to me. In one quick motion, he flipped the handle of the scissors into the palm of his hand and aimed the sharp end at my neck. "Do you hear me? If you tell mom I did this, I'll cut your throat in your sleep. Or, maybe I'll cut mom's throat in her sleep, and then you'll have to live with that. It'll be all your fault."

"I won't tell," I whispered, trying not to move.

He left my room without another word and I, just as I had countless times before, flipped my light switch on and off while counting to one hundred. By the time my mom reached one hundred years old, I had reasoned, she would be ready to die, and I could stop keeping her alive. Later that night, as my mom tucked me into bed, I lied and told her I was playing beauty shop and decided to cut Dolly's hair. She lied and told me I did a great job, that her hair looked perfect.

"Faith?" LuAnne's voice cracked, "A penny for your thoughts?"

I drew in a deep breath. "I just had a memory from my childhood."

"A fond memory, I hope." Then in her casual way added, "I was thinking about death."

"That doesn't sound pleasant." I sat on the edge of her bed, aware of a burning in my stomach.

"Oh, but it is pleasant. Death is a natural part of life. One can't go through life and never think about death."

"I suppose that's true." I pushed my hair back from my face. "What about death were you thinking?"

"Just that I'm ready."

"LuAnne . . ."

"Faith, I've lived a good life. A happy life. Shouldn't it be good to reach a place where death is welcomed and not dreaded?"

Goosebumps covered my skin.

"I know what you're thinking." She whispered, taking my hand. "That you'll miss me when I'm not here."

I sat quiet, searching her soft face. I already missed her when she wasn't here.

"On days like today, I feel fine." She widened her eyes, "I feel normal. But, we both know what's happening."

I felt a tear trickle down my cheek; it was becoming, to my dismay, increasingly difficult to control my tears. They seemed to sit on the edge, ever ready to leap. I turned my head and pressed my shoulder against my chin, soaking up the salty drop.

"Remember that broach my mother left me when she died?"

"It's your favorite."

"Yesterday I found it in the microwave oven." She looked at me and tilted her head to one side. "It's starting."

Her mother's broach in the microwave was a small finding compared to the mishaps that led us to begin moving her to an assisted living facility. What broke my heart the most was that to her, this was new; to her, it was just starting.

"You're sick, LuAnne, but you're not dying."

"We're born dying." She said with a chuckle. "I suppose what I'm saying is that, well, what am I without my mind? All I'm saying is that I'm ready for whatever comes. I'm good and ready. And I think that's the way it's supposed to be." LuAnne was wearing the same dainty pearl necklace she had worn every day since I first met her. She ran her fingers over the small white clumps the way she always had when troubled; the trouble that can only be worked out with a perpetual motion like tapping fingers or bouncing legs to keep the thoughts steady. Finally, she stood, still fingering the pearls and said, "Let's get packing, shall we?"

I worked at a supermarket bagging groceries when I was in high school. I rather enjoyed it, as simple as it was; I liked the challenge of putting as much as possible in a bag without making it too heavy and without compromising the softness of bread or the crunch of chips. Groceries were important, I would tell myself. I was packing items that were essential to sustaining life. I was reminded of this while helping LuAnne pack up her house because, in many ways, I was doing the same thing. I was packing up her memories which would, I thought, sustain her, and in time, sustain the rest of us.

"You don't have to do this, you know. You could always live with us."

"Pish posh," she said, waving her hand at me. "You don't really want that, and neither do I. Besides, how will you write this book about your brother if you're spending all day fussing over me?"

"You know about the book?"

"Wesley told me. He thinks it's an unfair request. And maybe it is, after all, he's only been dead for what? A month?"

"Three months," I said softly.

"Remember in *Little Women*? The movie, not the book, I've never read the book, and not the original movie but the one with that actress. You know, the one who acted all sweet in the movie, but she grew up to be a shoplifter?"

"Winona Ryder."

"Yes, that's the one. Winona. I've always liked that name. Anyway, remember in that movie . . ."

"*Little Women.*"

"Yes. Winona keeps giving her stories to that foreigner man for him to read, and he always likes them, but finally, he tells her that she could do so much more, write so much more, if she were brave enough to write what she knows, to write from the heart. Do you remember that?"

"Yes, I remember."

"Okay." She stood smiling at me.

"Okay," I repeated. "Okay, what?"

"Okay. You're Winona, and I'm the foreigner man. I'm telling you that I've liked everything you've ever written. But you could do so much more. If you're brave enough to write what you know, to write from your heart. This book, this book about your brother. This could be your so much more."

My so much more. These words fluttered around my head the entire day. With every drawer I opened, the words, all jumbled together, flew out like trapped moths. Every box I filled and taped shut seemed to rattle and knock about, the words not wanting to be trapped inside, the words: my so much more. The worst part was, she was right. While there is truth in all my work, pieces of myself in each character, my scent lingering in every fictional room, it was still fiction. In all my stories, I had disguised my fears, my joys, my good deeds, and murderous thoughts by attaching them to someone else; someone we all knew to be a figment of my imagination. But this, to achieve *my* so much more, would mean stepping out from behind my characters and showing my real self. People would read about my brother and see not only what I had done but what had been done to me. They would then point to my other works and say, "Oh, now we know why she wrote that . . . this character clearly represents so and so." My readers would speculate, scrutinize, and make assumptions about my work, and suddenly I would be more than a writer to them, more than an entertainer; I would be real, and the thought of it all made me feel sick inside. I've allowed people to see what I wanted them to see. LuAnne was asking me to expose myself, my full self. To reveal the dust hiding in the corners and the muck that has seeped down in the crevices.

What about that was so much more? I was happy with my quiet life. I was happy with my so little less.

By the time I drove home, with Finn in the back seat reciting the details of his day, I realized my face was actually sore. I had been squinting and pushing my eyebrows together all day, thinking about those words. Those words, the foreigner man's words, had made my face hurt and had undoubtedly given me new, irreversible wrinkles.

I dropped my purse in its usual spot as we walked in the front door. Finn went to his room, bounding up the stairs with energy to spare. I went to the bookshelf in the den and ran my fingers over the books that held stories I'd written, over the books that held stories written by better authors than myself, and then over photo albums which held our memories, the documentation of life. I slid one album from its place and opened it to find Sadie as a newborn wrapped in a fuzzy blanket. Wes held her tiny face next to his and his smile said it all. He loved her. I flipped through the pages slowly, taking in all the photos. She was so beautiful. So smart. But, there was something about her. Something about her in every picture, something in her eyes that said something wasn't right. Like she knew all along.

I couldn't help but grab the next album and the next. I needed to see the progression of Sadie's life, the addition of Finn. I needed to see Wes go from late nights of patrol to being police chief. I needed to see myself go from a wife struggling with infertility to a mother of one, then of two. I needed to see how happy we all looked. I needed to know there was once happiness, that there was more before my brother died. I noticed as I flipped through the pages of the albums that he wasn't in any of the pictures, my brother. I thought I had managed to keep him out of our lives. But, as I thought back over all the pictures, pieces of him were on every page.

At dinner that night, we sat quietly while we ate. Perhaps it was time to break the silence and push us back to where we once were.

"Finn," I said softly, "How was your day at school?"

"I already told you all about it. Saying it all again would be redundant."

Wes chuckled, Sadie rolled her eyes, and I bit my lip.

"Sadie," I said, even softer, "I hear there's a college and career night coming up. Should we go? See what colleges you might be interested—"

"I'm not going to college," she interrupted. "I have no plans for college or for a career."

Wes sat up straight in his chair. I regretted not liking our new normal.

She went on, "Money's not an issue, so I think when I'm done with high school—if I finish high school—I might just travel. I might be one of those gypsy types who just backpacks from one country to another, never really settling down. That's my current plan."

Wes and I exchanged glances. Finn pointed his fork at Sadie and with a full mouth said, "That sounds dumb."

Sadie leaned in towards Finn and pushed her eyebrows together, "Dumb? Really? The best you can do is *dumb*?"

"Sadie," I said slowly, "take a deep breath."

Ignoring me, she leaned even further over the table. "Come on Finn, why not say I'm being ludicrous?" Her chin-length hair hugged her face, and she quickly tucked both sides behind her ears.

"I like the word *dumb*."

"Yeh, well using the word *dumb* makes you sound dumb."

"That's enough," Wes scolded.

"I'm just trying to help!" she belted, "You don't want Finn to be dumb do you?"

"Sadie, that's enough," Wes's voice, like thunder, radiated across the table.

"Right," Sadie snapped, "That's enough." She pushed her chair back and the legs rubbed against the floor making a farting noise that would normally have made us all laugh.

"Dumb's a valid word." Finn said swallowing hard, "Besides, what's dumb is that your cello won't fit in a backpack. You'll have to learn the harmonica or something." Sadie stood staring at Finn from across the table, her hands in fists. "Dumb's a valid word." He said again.

There could have been more words; words that would have cut deep and kept us up all night, but to protect Finn, we kept our mouths shut and let Sadie storm up the stairs. As her bedroom door slammed shut, I found myself staring at Finn. He caught me staring and grinned, a bit of potato stuck to the side of his mouth. There was something in his eyes too, but something different than Sadie's. He didn't know. Not yet anyway. He didn't know the message being sent by the haunting sounds of the cello that slid under Sadie's door and down the stairs, or why they wrapped themselves around my neck, squeezing so tight I could hardly breathe.

I stared at the food on my plate, pushing bits and pieces around not even trying to raise the fork to my mouth; my throat was too constricted to swallow. Wes and Finn cleaned their plates—men's appetites rarely being spoiled—and the instant they left the table I thought about gathering the tablecloth at its four corners and throwing it all away. That seemed easier than loading the dishwasher. But, eventually, we'd run out of dishes, and I didn't have time to buy more. So, as Wes reclined with his feet propped up, reading the headlines on his laptop, and Finn curled up on the sofa with a book, I went about doing what needed to be done, feeling incredibly lonely. Sadie would normally be sitting at the bar doing her homework, chatting with me as I loaded the dishwasher, but that was before. Now I stood in the kitchen watching Wes and

Finn, and I couldn't help but think that the open floor plan we intentionally chose to keep our family connected seemed pointless.

"Finn, what are you reading?"

I knew he wouldn't answer me until he got to a good stopping place, so I waited.

"*The Boys of Botswana.*" He let out a breath and lowered the book, so I could see his face. "It's about two boys who are on a safari with their parents. They get separated and the boys, they didn't know each other before, become instant best friends, and not just for the sake of surviving, but like for real best friends."

"Do they find their parents?" I asked.

"I don't know yet, Mom. I just started reading it." He put his book back up to eye level. Wes smiled at me and shook his head. I rubbed my eyebrow, as it wouldn't stop twitching, and then went back to cleaning the kitchen—back to feeling lonely. When Sadie finally stopped protesting through her cello, Finn went to his room and Wes changed for his nightly run.

"Exercise would help your stress level too," he said, pulling me into his arms. I noted that he was one of those men that made neon green running shorts look sexy, not ridiculous.

"I only run if someone's chasing me," I said, resting my head on his chest.

"I'll chase you if you want." He teased, lightly smacking my back side. "Really, come with me. It would do you good to get some fresh air."

The words in my mind were mean and unreasonable, "I hate running as much as I hate fresh air. Fresh air just reminds me of happier days. Days we may never get back. Fresh air makes me feel like I'm suffocating."

The words that came out of my mouth were thankful and loving. "Thank you, honey. I know you're right. When I get your mom settled, I'll start exercising again. Just a few more days. Besides, I'm okay. Really."

"You're not okay."

"Why do say that?"

"Because I know you." He studied my face for a moment. I wondered if he could hear me thinking that he, in fact, doesn't know me as well as he thinks he does. "Moving my mom would be enough to stress anyone out. Then add Sadie on top of it . . . it's no wonder . . ."

"It's no wonder what?" I asked.

"I just know you're not okay. And neither am I. But, we'll get through this."

Wes lifted my chin and kissed me. A soft, slow, drawn out kiss that made me feel like my body and soul were separating. Like part of me was drifting away.

"I'm sorry," he whispered, his lips still touching mine.

"For what?" I asked, my eyes still closed, my legs off balance.

"For not helping with the move." I opened my eyes to find tears in his. "I just can't . . ."

"I know," I whispered. And I did know. Moving his mom into River Side was accepting realities he wasn't ready to accept. Letting go of his childhood home was closing a chapter he wasn't ready to close. He put his head on my shoulder and took a cleansing breath.

"You know, Faith, I spend most of my days dealing with domestic disputes. That and narcotics." He stood up straight and wiped his eyes with the palms of his hands. "I know things seem tough right now. But, there are families in this town that would trade places with us in a heartbeat. We have to keep that in mind. Or, I do, anyway."

We stood, facing one another; a swirl of unspoken words between us. I often forget that Wes carries the burdens of this town, not just those of our family. I wonder now if he ever wants to just keep running, as fast and as far away as possible. I would never ask, of course. And he would never tell.

"Go," I told him.

"We'll get through this," he said again. "Partners?" he asked with a wink.

"Through thick and thin," I winked back.

Wes brushed the back of his fingers across my cheek as he stepped away. He stopped at the front door to tighten his laces, blew me a kiss, and then stepped out into the cool night air.

As I drug myself up the stairs, I thought about how in movies when people fight, they usually show a scene with one person sitting on a bed or on the edge of the bathtub, usually crying. Another person stands on the opposite side of the closed door, softly touching it, desperately wanting a connection with the person they're fighting with. This is what I thought of as I stood outside Sadie's door, my hand flat against it. I pictured her sitting on her bed, crying. I rested my forehead against her door, hoping that at any moment she would open the door and send me falling to the floor. It would give us something to laugh about. But she didn't open her door, so I just stood there: remembering. Not long ago, Sadie would get chatty at bedtime. She would laugh and tell me funny things that happened at school. She would tell me about her boyfriend, Kyle; whatever he had done that day that had either made her love him or hate him. She talked about the things that seemed deep at her age; things I didn't always understand but still loved hearing about, simply because she wanted to tell me. I knew that would change. I knew having my sixteen-year-old still confide in me was something special, and I always felt like I was on borrowed time. I soaked up every minute, every conversation. And now, here we were, barely speaking—a closed door between us. I pressed both hands against her door and whispered, "I love you." If this were a movie, she would either whisper the same, sweet words back to me or throw her pillow, or perhaps a lamp, at the door and curse at me. I didn't hear any movement, so I told myself she whispered back, *I love you.*

At my desk I sat, once again, staring at a blank page with nothing, absolutely nothing, coming to mind. It's as if words have hidden themselves from me or erased themselves from my memory so that my brain has to ask, "Words? What are words?" My inability to push letters together is absurd. After all, I wasn't being asked to make something up, like on those reality shows when they hand you a box of random ingredients and have you bake a cake from scratch with mayonnaise instead of butter. Baking under those circumstances, making something up (like writing fiction), is laborsome. While I would never say this to the face of a nonfiction writer, I assumed writing about my brother would be as easy as opening a box mix, adding the eggs and oil, and tossing it in the oven. But, that hadn't been the case. Writing about my brother redefined my understanding of laborsome. Perhaps one day I *would* say that to the face of a nonfiction writer. Confess my ignorance. Offer to buy them a stiff drink.

My logic, which would prove to be faulty, was that if fiction freely flowed out of me in the a.m., perhaps nonfiction would freely flow in the p.m. It was this logic that had me sitting at my laptop staring at the cursor that blinked restlessly on the empty white page. It might have, after all, been better to join Wes on his run.

With a defeated sigh, I minimized my document and opened the browser. I would search for biographies and get an idea of how to go about this. I typed in Johnny Cash, then said to myself, "He wasn't a saint by any means, but he was too likable." I deleted his name. "I need an unlikable person." Quickly, and with force, I searched Adolf Hitler, then decided that was taking it a little too far. Then, out of curiosity, I entered my brother's name. In the blink of an eye images of his face were forming before me, and with one fell swoop I clicked the tiny x in the corner, slapped the laptop closed, and jumped from my chair. I realized I was shaking my hands, as if air drying them, when I stepped out in the hallway.

With my hands shoved in the back pockets of my jeans, I found Finn sitting up in bed, his nose buried in a book. I sat next to him and waited till he carefully placed his Darth Vader bookmark in its place and slide the book under his covers, patting it gently, as if tucking it in for the night.

"Did you brush?"

He answered by baring his teeth like a mad man.

"Did you wash behind your ears?"

"Squeaky clean," he answered.

I leaned in to kiss his forehead but was distracted by an offensive—

"Finn, what is that smell?"

"You don't wanna know."

"No, really. I think I do. I think I should know."

"Dad said you won't want to know."

"Then I definitely think I should know."

Finn sighed as deeply as a nine-year-old boy can sigh, flopped himself over the side of his bed, and from underneath pulled out a paper plate with a moldy peanut butter and jelly sandwich.

"Oh, Finn." I leaned back, not wanting to inhale the invisible floating particles. "This had better be an experiment."

"It is," he beamed. "I don't know why I didn't think of it before. I was reading about Alexander Fleming—excuse me," he widened his eyes and shook his head, "Sir Alexander Fleming. Anyway, he discovered penicillin from some stuff that had gone moldy. How many lives do you think he's saved, Mom? Huh? How many?"

"I have no idea."

"The number is astronomical. It's incalculable." This last word he stumbled over, giving it extra syllables.

"Okay," I said, taking the paper plate and setting it on the floor out of reach, "So what? Are you hoping to find a new strand of lifesaving mold?"

"Exactly! I was thinking I'd put it in a baggy, and sometime when I'm with Grandma and her brain isn't working right, I'll pull some out and blow it in her face."

"Finn . . ."

"No, really. Inhaling it makes sense, don't you think? I mean, your nostrils are so close to your brain."

"I don't think it works that way."

"Maybe not. I'll do more research, but I think I'm on to something."

"You're onto something alright." I kissed Finn's forehead through his thick bangs, picked up the plate of mold and said, "I'm taking this with me. But, keep researching. I'm super impressed." With a wink and a nod, I turned off his light.

"You're not gonna throw that away are you?"

"Finn, honey . . ."

"Mom, I worked so hard on it."

In my head, I said, "Right, you worked so hard. You made a PB&J, put it on a paper plate, and slid it under your bed. That's crazy hard work. Try telling that to Sir Alexander Fleming." Out loud I said, "I'll tell you what. I'll go put this in a ziplock bag, and we'll figure it out in the morning. Deal?"

"Deal."

I imagine Finn was fast asleep before I made it to the kitchen to bag his moldy sandwich and wash my hands three times to remove all the invisible particles. We all said it was his superpower: the ability to fall asleep before his head hit the pillow. The kid could sleep anywhere, anytime. Something I envied about him. He didn't lie awake at night making to-do lists in his head, planning meals, and figuring out how to fit thirty-six hours worth of tasks into a twenty-four hour day and still get some sleep. He didn't lie awake at night wondering and worrying. While I did envy this about him, I wanted this for him: wonder and worry. If he never lies awake at night wondering and worrying, it will likely mean he has no one in his life that he loves. But that's the funny thing about love, in the moments of joy and peace, love is all there is. In the moments of wonder and worry, you can't help but question if love is worth it, because the joy and peace seem so far away, unreachable.

By the time I made it back upstairs, because it seems a woman can never enter a kitchen to do one task and only actually do a single task, Wes was back from his run, freshly showered and sitting up in bed, waiting for me. I closed our door and shed my clothes as I crossed the room and slid under the covers next to him. Over the past several months our lovemaking had become something different, something desperate. It was a form of comfort for me, an escape, *my* nightly run. He allowed me this, and I loved him for it. I loved him for letting me lose myself in him, and then for holding me and letting me cry after.

That night, after the crying had stopped, we moved away from one another and into our sleeping spots. I could hear the wind outside, a reminder that fall was creeping in. I made a mental note to check Finn's closet to see if he needed new fall and winter pants, his legs seemed to get longer every day. In the darkness I could picture the leaves falling from the trees; I could almost smell them as they crunched underfoot. I took in a deep breath and for a moment found myself smiling, but then it happened; reality came back to mind, as it never stayed gone for long.

"Can you sleep?" Wes whispered, finding my hand under the covers.

"Probably not."

"I don't like falling asleep before you—I feel like I'm leaving you behind."

I smiled, squeezed his hand, and ached inside as he did just that, leave me behind. He drifted into that place—that place that's unique to each of us—while I stayed behind. Eventually, my thoughts would become so jumbled and distorted I would have no choice but to be ushered into my other place full of hauntings. The deepest, darkest of places. However, until that inevitably came, I would stay awake, as had become my habit, till the wee hours replaying the last three months of our lives. I would think, regret, wonder, and worry.

On this particular night, I sat up in bed with my laptop balanced on my legs, and after what seemed like hours of searching unlikable celebrities, I came across an article that would send me on a path towards my something more. I just didn't know it yet. The article was about an older woman who had spent most of her adult life traveling the world working as a humanitarian. When her health began to decline, she returned to America and decided to write her memoirs. Every day she dedicated time to sitting, remembering, and writing; titling each memory to give them individual attention. When she wrote the last line of the last memory she hugged the pages to her chest and smiled with deep satisfaction. A few weeks later she decided to read over the stories herself before handing them over to an editor, and after doing so, she was shocked at what she had written.

She had not started her story by recounting her first fundraiser that would send her to Haiti with a group of her high school friends. Instead, she started with the first fundraiser for her sister, who was a child prodigy of sorts, to purchase a piano. She didn't spend much time describing her year-long stay in Bagdad. Instead, she described herself sitting in her bunker reading a letter from her sister who had been accepted to Julliard. Page after page it became more clear that she was not the main character in her own story, her sister was.

Discouraged, and admittedly embarrassed, she canceled her meeting with the editor, put the pages in a binder, put the binder on a shelf, and left them there to collect dust. It wasn't until several years later when her sister, who had become a world renowned concert pianist, died in a plane crash that she would pull those pages off the shelf and seek publication.

In this interview, she admitted that if she had been asked *after* her sister died to share these memories, none of them would have come to mind. At least she doubted they would have. It took her writing her own story to realize how much her sister had impacted her life and how much their lives, though lived mostly in different countries, were intertwined. Her story was her sister's, and her sister's story was hers.

She regretted, deeply regretted, not publishing these memories while her sister was alive and could enjoy them. But now they would serve as a reminder of a life well lived and would hopefully keep her sister 's memory alive after she herself was gone.

As I sat, reading this interview, I realized I had found my inspiration. I would stop trying to write about my brother. I would instead write about myself. Because my life was his, and his was mine. If it worked for this woman, why wouldn't it work for me? If I wrote my own memoirs, my brother would show his ugly face in everything; there was no question about that. The real question was, how could I write this story and leave Sadie out of it?

Gidget

My parents bought a new house when I was ten years old. When we pulled into the driveway, I remember my mother saying, "Oh, it's even prettier than I remembered." She looked at my father with a big smile and whispered, "It's perfect."

My cheeks went hot, not from what my mother had said, but because of the twinkle in my dad's eye when he looked at her and nodded. I folded my lips between my teeth to keep from smiling.

I climbed out of our minivan and ran up the stairs of the front porch and, to my surprise, curled up beside the front door was a calico cat. The cat looked up and started purring the instant our eyes met. Gidget, the name I gave her on the spot, stood, stretched, and then curled herself around my ankles. "I guess she comes with the house." My dad said as he unlocked the door. "I can keep her?" I squealed. He merely nodded with that same twinkle in his eye, and I felt my cheeks go hot again.

Because to a child, there is no time—life just happens as it happens—I circled our new home, collecting sticks and twigs for what might have been ten minutes or five hours; I'll never know for sure. I had decided to build Gidget her own little house, and, for a moment, I thought about making it big enough for two cats, should she ever decide to invite a friend over. But, then I concluded that that's the sort of thing a seven-year-old would do, not a ten-year-old. Cats don't invite friends over.

Gidget followed my every step—sometimes so closely I stepped on her—and every so often she would plop down, roll over, and rub her back against the ground. I would then put my bundle down and pat her belly making her kick at my arm with her hind legs and wrap her front paws around my hand, pulling my fingers to her mouth. Gidget would lick, bite, and gnaw on my fingertips, and I would speak softly to her, telling her how pretty she was and that I would take care of her, that she could count on me. She, of course, had no idea how good I was at taking care of people. My parents, for instance, were alive because of me.

After collecting what seemed like the perfect amount of supplies, Gidget and I settled on the front porch and began constructing her new home. It only took a matter of minutes, of course, before I realized the thin wood pieces wouldn't hold themselves together.

So I circled the house a second time, plucking the tallest blades of grass I could find and any long stems from weeds growing in the cracks. I labored over attaching the twigs until finally I had a small structure loosely leaning against the house. "Here," I said to Gidget, "This is for you!" She stood and stretched again because she had been watching me build, and watching for a cat is just as exhausting as building. When Gidget came closer, I realized the house was only large enough for one of her legs, no way could her entire body fit inside and no way, no how could she invite a friend over— not that she would, because cats don't do that.

At ten years old I was furious with my limitations. At that moment, with Gidget pawing at my feet trying for my attention, I realized I wasn't able to do what I wanted to do. I needed wood, real wood. I needed a hammer and nails. I needed a saw and paint. I needed a grown up. I needed help. And that made me furious. It was my mom who came to the rescue with an empty box and an old towel. It wasn't the palace I had pictured in my head, but it would do. It was my dad who suggested I use markers and decorate the box. It was my brother who held Gidget ransom anytime he wanted something from me. I protected Gidget, as I did my parents, without her knowing. The love I had for her seemed worth the sacrifice, even at the age of ten.

A year later I tripped over a tree root while playing kickball at recess. The school nurse concluded I hadn't broken any bones but had what was likely a slight concussion from hitting my head. A call to our family doctor gave us peace of mind, but my brother whispered in my ear after dinner that people with concussions often died in their sleep, if I was smart, he said, I'd stay awake all night.

At bedtime, I asked my mother if she would sleep in my bed for the night. If I died, I wanted her with me.

"You don't need me to sleep with you," she said, kissing my forehead.

"But, I do. My head hurts really bad." I was lying of course, but she obliged.

We crawled into bed, both of us on our sides facing each other. She started rubbing my head and playing with my hair, humming almost inaudibly.

"Do you think I have brain damage?" I finally managed to ask.

"No," she chuckled. "I don't think you have brain damage."
"What if when I grow up, my brain doesn't work right and I can't do all the things I want to do?" I was trying hard not to cry.

"Faith, I don't know what's going to happen to you between now and the time you grow up. But, what happened to you today did not hurt your brain. Your brain is fine. As of now, you can grow up and do anything you want to do." She said this with as much compassion as she could muster at the end of an exhausting day. Then she added, "Tell me all the things you'd like to do when you grow up."

"I want to be a mom," I told her.

She smiled and caressed my cheek. Her hand was soft and warm. "Being a mom is very hard work," she whispered. "But, I think you'd be great at it."

"When you were my age, what did you want to be?" I asked through a yawn.

"A teacher. I always wanted to be a teacher. And a mom. I always wanted to be a mom."

"Why is being a mom hard work?" I asked, my words distorted by another yawn.

She hesitated, held her breath for a moment, then said, "Maybe it won't be so hard for you. Hush now, you need sleep. It's been a long day."

"I can't sleep."

"Well, you won't sleep if you keep talking."

"I need to keep talking. I need to stay awake. I'm afraid if I . . ."

"If you what?"

"I'm afraid if I sleep . . . I might not wake up."

"Faith," she said my name as if I were eight, not eleven. "Why wouldn't you wake up?"

"I read somewhere," another lie, "that people with concussions sometimes die in their sleep."

"Where did you read that?" She raised her eyebrows while waiting for my answer.

"I don't remember."

"You're not going to die in your sleep. You have nothing to be afraid of."

I did of course, have something to be afraid of. In fact, I had lots of things to be afraid of. I wanted to tell her that. I wanted to tell her everything there was to tell. But, I didn't. She was tracing invisible lines on my face now, and as much as I wanted to stay awake, I couldn't keep my eyes open. She started humming again and in those moments, as my eyes lazily opened and closed, I admired her smooth skin and the perfect arch in her eyebrows. If I was going to die, I wanted to remember her face, to take that memory with me. As I closed my eyes for the last time, I decided that dying was okay. I was with someone who loved me. And that made it okay.

It was in the wee hours of the morning that I heard my door open and felt someone standing over me. I was pleasantly surprised to still be alive and even more so to realize my mother was still in bed with me. I listened to her voice say, "What are you doing in here? Are you sleepwalking?" I felt her sit up in bed. "Wake up. Hey, wake up. Go back to your room." He never said a word, but I heard the floor creak as he hurried out, closing the door behind him. The next morning as I walked into the kitchen I heard my dad say, "Really? Sleepwalking? I wonder how often he does that."

"Should we take him to the doctor?" Mom questioned.

He cleared his throat and asked with confidence, "What for? What can they do for sleepwalking?"

After breakfast, as was my habit, I went out on the front porch to feed Gidget, but to my surprise, she wasn't there. I snapped my fingers, which was my usual way to get her attention, but she still didn't come.

"Mom? Have you seen Gidget?"

"She's always waiting for you in the mornings, is she not there?"

I walked around the house calling her name, but she was nowhere to be found.

School was miserable that day; I couldn't concentrate on anything. I watched the hands on the clock, willing them to 2:45 so I could go home and search for her. But, Gidget was never to be seen again, and that's the day I started snapping my fingers six times, six times a day. Because there were six letters in Gidget's name, I convinced myself that if I snapped my fingers six times, six times a day, she would come home. But, of course, she didn't. It took me almost six years to realize that no amount of snapping was going to bring her back. And so I've learned over the years, in adulthood, that no amount of anything within my power can protect anyone. This truth kept me crying myself to sleep as a child, and I admit, sometimes still as an adult.

2

Tuesday

By six o'clock, I was out of bed and at my computer. At seven, I was reading over memory #1 for the hundredth time, feeling a bit more numb with each read when I noticed Finn standing at the door staring at me.

"I'm supposed to bring cookies to school today."

"And you're just telling me now, Finn?"

"I forgot."

"It's not like you to forget."

Slowly and with care, he said, "I've been distracted."

"By what?"

"Life."

What do you say to a nine-year-old who says he's distracted by life? Finn glanced down the hall towards Sadie's bedroom.

"Finn, what's going on? Is Sadie bothering you?"

"She's not bothering me. She's distracting me."

"How is she distracting you?"

He said in an almost whisper, "I can hear her crying at night. It wakes me up. A few days ago I asked her what was wrong, and she said something really ambiguous, and then she told me to leave her alone. So now I spend my nights listening to her cry and my days wondering what she's crying about, and it's distracting. Anyway, I have to take cookies to school today. Homemade would have been preferable, but at this point, if we leave a little early, we can stop at the store on the way." He walked away, leaving me alone, staring at the empty door frame, my heart caught in my throat.

I found Sadie sitting in her usual spot at the kitchen counter. I tried to sound casual as if last night hadn't happened.

"Can I make you some breakfast? Eggs, toast?"

"Not hungry."

"Is everything okay?"

"I told you yesterday; it's just PMS."

Before I could say another word, she was on her feet leaving the room.

"Good morning, sweetheart," I heard Wes say to her as they passed in the hallway. Sadie didn't respond. He rushed into the kitchen, shaking his head. "Still brooding, I see."

"She hates me," I whispered, burying my head in his chest.

"She hates us both." He stepped back, giving me a quick kiss. "It'll get easier." He kissed me again, grabbed his keys, and headed out.

"Wes, wait." I followed him, noticing how handsome he looked in uniform. "Have you used the word *ambiguous* lately?"

"Ambiguous? Why would I use the word *ambiguous*?"

"Never mind."

He kissed me again, quickly, then stopped to hold my gaze long enough to make me smile, and then he left.

I sent Sadie into the supermarket to buy cookies. She returned with a bag of Oreos and tossed them in Finn's lap. Homemade cookies would have been preferable, but Oreos would have to do. *I've become that mom*, I thought to myself.

"Finn, give me warning next time, will you? I'd gladly make homemade cookies." Finn sat, lost in his own little world: him, Batman, and a bag of Oreo cookies.

Sadie sat next to me rubbing her forehead.

"This is a bad month, huh?"

"You can say that again," Sadie whispered.

"This is a bad month, huh?" Finn said from the backseat. "Good one, huh, Sadie?" Sadie ignored him, but he and I exchanged grins in the mirror.

"Did you take something?" I tried to feel her forehead, but she moved her head away. "I'm not sure you should go to school today."

She stared out her window; her breathing was shallow. She turned to face me and with hollow eyes said, "Please leave me alone."

When we reached the high school, Sadie slid off her seat and out of the car, she trudged towards her friend, Claire, who was waiting on the sidewalk.

"Sadie's perplexing," Finn said, watching his sister. "Oh, wait. I just learned the word *sullen*. I could also say that Sadie's sullen."

"Indeed," I said, suddenly aware that one day he would learn a word that best describes me.

"She's been this way since Uncle—"

"I know." I interrupted, not wanting to hear his name.

He went on, "It doesn't make any sense. We hardly knew him. Why's she so sad?"

"Death is sad, even if you don't know the person very well."

"Does death have to be sad? I mean, what if you're really old or really sick, and you're ready to die? Can't death be a good thing?"

"Yes," I told him, and instantly my arms and legs began to tingle, a dismal sensation that has become a frequent visitor.

Before climbing out of the car, Finn leaned forward between the seats. "Don't sweat the Oreos." He said, then noticing the baggie of mold sticking out of my purse, "Oh great, are you gonna blow that in Grandma's face today?"

"Umm, no. No, I'm not going to blow mold in Grandma's face."

"Mom, it's in the name of science. Don't you want her to get better?"

"How about I put a little in her coffee when she's not looking?"

He looked up out of the corner of his eyes. "Okay. That could work. I'll want a full report at dinner."

"Will do."

And that was that. Finn walked into the school building with a skip in his step, fully believing his mother was going to put mold from a PB&J into his grandmother's coffee in hopes of curing her Alzheimer's.

When I left LuAnne's house the day before, she was emotional about cleaning out Vernon's closet, something we should have done three years ago. I left her standing before his neatly hung wardrobe, telling her to get some rest, and we would tackle it tomorrow. It was now tomorrow, and I found her standing before his closet with a nervous, childlike determination; one hand on her hip, the other on her pearls.

"We should do this now," she said quickly. "I'm through crying about it. It must be done."

"Yes," I agreed. "It must be done."

We removed his clothing piece by piece, taking time for her to touch and smell each one. His shirts were starched to a crisp and his slacks were ironed with a sharp crease down the front. His neckties hung neatly in a row, arranged by color, most of them gifts from Sadie and Finn. I told Vernon once that out of all the lawyers in town, he was the best dressed. He told me that out of all his daughter-in-laws, I was his favorite.

"Look at all those neckties. Why do you suppose he collected neckties?" LuAnne held a bundle of them in her hands. "I was going to give his clothes to the Goodwill. I thought maybe some homeless person could use them. But now that I look at them. Well, what homeless person would want to dress like a lawyer?"

"I shop at Goodwill, and I'm not homeless," I told her.

"Well, but why would you buy these? Why would you wear men's clothing and dress like a lawyer?"

"Would you like me to take these to Vernon's office and see if his partners could use them?"

She blinked several times. "Yes. That seems like a good idea."

This was why LuAnne couldn't live alone anymore. Some days her mind was clearer and she spoke reasonably about life and what was happening to her. Other days she thought only homeless people shopped at Goodwill.

As we sifted through the closets I was saddened that today, of all days, she wasn't all there. I wanted her to experience the memories. I wanted her to remember the dress she wore on their 50th wedding anniversary. I wanted her to remember the hideous, tie- dyed scarf Finn had given her for her 60th birthday. I wanted, so badly, for her to remember. So, I remembered for her. I smiled, chuckled and teared up on her behalf as I folded and tucked away her treasures.

"LuAnne, do you remember this one?"

"No," she said quietly and went back to folding and refolding the box of sweaters in front of her.

"That's okay," I whispered. "I remember."

When Finn was two weeks old, LuAnne came to our house and asked to take me shopping. Shopping? Wes couldn't believe his ears. She wanted to take me shopping, just for a bit, just while Finn was napping. We'd be home soon. LuAnne took me to a clothing store in a neighboring town, her favorite boutique, she said.

"Pick out anything you want," she beamed. "Don't look at the price tag, do you hear me? I just want you to find something that makes you feel good about yourself, and then I would like to buy it for you."

I had learned early on not to argue with LuAnne. Gifts were her love language and I would love her by allowing her to buy me something whether I needed it or not. I gave her a quick hug and began sifting through the racks of clothing.

I picked out a thin, black, cowl neck sweater. There was one tiny white bird embroidered near the bottom hem.

"How sad the bird looks," LuAnne noted.

"Yes," I agreed. "It's floating over a black expanse. I fear it won't find a place to land."

LuAnne stood still, looking at me then at the lonely bird embroidered on the bottom hem, then back at me.

"I love it," she finally said. "I absolutely love it. I think I need one too."

We wore the sweaters home that day and laughed when Wes asked to take our picture. "Faith . . . what have you done with my mother?" Wes scolded me from behind the camera. "My mom wears bright, cheerful colors. She always looks like spring. You've gone and turned her into another forlorn literary type."

"Pish posh," LuAnne said, waving her hand at him. "Black is not forlorn, it's classic."

"Thank you!" I said, raising my eyebrows and smirking at Wes.

"Classically forlorn." Wes teased, taking a candid picture.

LuAnne took my hand and said to Wes, very seriously, "Your wife is most comfortable in black because it reminds her of ink; the ink on the pages of the books she reads and writes. Black is comfortable, black is home."

I'm not sure I had ever smiled bigger than I did in that moment. Which is silly, really. But, I did. I smiled my biggest smile in that moment. Then, still holding my hand, LuAnne looked me in the eye and said in a low voice, "I don't look at this sweater and see a lonely bird. I see a brave bird. A bird that keeps flying because it has yet to find a safe place to land."

This memory was especially clear to me. Those pictures Wes took were in my photo album; I had seen them yesterday. I remember at the time feeling so lucky to have LuAnne as a mother-in-law. I was lucky because she saw me. She understood. And I loved her for this. I loved her then, and I loved her still—for this.

Vernon and LuAnne were much like my own parents, only more adult somehow.

I had confided in LuAnne, once upon a time, about how my brother had mistreated and misused me. She listened, as she always did, with complete concentration, unlike most people who, instead of listening, are immediately formulating their response, dismissing your opinions on the subject for their own. LuAnne took my hand and said she was sorry I had dealt with such terrible things at such a young age. She said *she* was sorry, though she had done nothing wrong.

"You never told your parents, did you?" she had asked.

"How did you know?"

"If they had known, they would have put a stop to it," LuAnne said softly.

She was right, of course. They would have stopped it had they known. But now LuAnne knew, and I'm confident she shared that piece of me with Vernon, not just because they had the kind of marriage that held no secrets, but because after that day he looked at me with even kinder eyes and hugged me in a more delicate, intentional way. My in-laws knew something about me that my own parents didn't know. I had always felt I was protecting my parents somehow, by keeping this from them. But in this memory, for the first time, I felt that my silence was a betrayal.

That day I roamed about LuAnne's house lost in thought, moving around boxes that had already been taped shut, and listening to her hum as she went from room to room. I wondered what would happen to this house. I pictured the young family that would soon be moving in and saw them being happy here, really happy. This house was sturdy, and if the walls could talk, they would tell stories of love and laughter and tears and sorrow. These walls had seen it all, heard it all. From Wes's birth to Vernon's death, these walls had held this family together, and in a matter of days we would no longer be welcomed here. The locks would be changed, and our keys would no longer work. I wanted the walls always to be beige and the carpet to be grayish blue with an orangish stain in the corner of the living room (a stain that no one remembers how it got there, it's just always been). I wanted the kitchen to forever smell like fresh coffee and for my nose to always burn from the potpourri bag in the coat closet. I wanted Vernon to still be alive and for LuAnne to not be sick and for my mind to not click a million miles per minute.

"I'll see you later." LuAnne stood in the doorway, clutching her purse.

"Are you going somewhere?" I asked.

"I'd really like some ice cream. I think I'll go and get some."

"I'll take you."

"No need," she smiled sweetly. "I'll call Loopy."

"Loopy?"

"My driver." She said this with the arrogance of a sixteen-year-old. "From the Senior Transport Service." I half expected her to add a "duh" at the end of her sentence.

I took a deep breath. Reminded myself I was talking to LuAnne and not Sadie.

"Lupe. Yes, I've met Lupe."

"It's Loopy. That's how he says it. He says his name is Loopy."

"I believe you. But, I think it's actually pronounced Lupe."

"Then why would he say his name is Loopy? Lupe makes him sound Italian. He's not Italian."

"Well, he's probably used to us . . . non-Hispanic people . . . pronouncing it wrong, so he probably just gave up, and thought it was easier to just say it the way we say it."

LuAnne pondered this for a moment. "I don't think so." She concluded. "I can say Lupe just as easily as Loopy. Besides, it's . . . bad to think we're so . . . bad at words that we can't learn to say his name right. But, anyway, you're wrong. He's not Italian."

"I know he's not Italian."

"Then why are you giving him a name from . . . that place where Italian people are from?"

There was a pregnant pause. The air in the house felt stagnant even though we'd been moving around, disturbing the atmosphere for hours. Finally, I wiped the back of my hand across my forehead and said over-energetically, "Boy, I'm really hot from all this work. I'd sure love some ice cream."

"Maybe Loopy will give you a ride too."

"LuAnne, how about we don't call Loopy, and I'll drive us to get ice cream."

She stood like a statue considering this option.

"I don't want you to come with me and then be upset when we get back that there's still work to be done."

"LuAnne, I won't be upset. There's plenty of time to get this done. I would really like to take you to get ice cream."

"I would really like you to ask Loopy how to say his name."

I hung my head and could feel the tension building between my shoulder blades.

"I'm sure you're right, LuAnne. I was wrong. If he said his name is Loopy, then his name is Loopy."

At Tasty Freeze, LuAnne ordered "nuttercrunch," and I mouthed "butterscotch" to the waitress, to which she simply smiled and nodded. LuAnne told the waitress that nuttercrunch had been her favorite since she was a little girl, to which the waitress smiled and nodded. I ordered vanilla and thought of all the times Sadie had teased me saying, "Vanilla's boring. Live a little; at least get vanilla and chocolate swirl." Finn would remind Sadie, "Mom's not boring, she's plain." To which I would smile and nod. I licked my vanilla cone and thought of how many times I had kindly explained to Sadie that vanilla isn't boring. Vanilla is for people who have lived long enough and experienced enough of life to know that real pleasure is found in the simple things. Sadie would grin at me with a sympathetic look in her eye; as if she knew what there was to know about me.

Maybe I was boring, plain. Maybe it wasn't that life had taught me to enjoy the simple things, maybe life had taught me not to trust anything new, to only rely on what I knew to be safe. Maybe I had surrounded myself with vanilla because vanilla held no surprises; you couldn't hide anything in a blob of white. I told myself that next time I would have something different, like chocolate and vanilla swirl—baby steps towards something like butterscotch or chocolate peanut butter.

I watched LuAnne enjoy her ice cream, licking it with the satisfaction of a child. I handed her a napkin when her chin needed cleaning and was thankful, for her sake, that she understood. I understood, due to her excessive yawning on the drive home, that she needed a nap.

"These need mailing." She said to me, pulling a thin stack of envelopes out of her purse as we pulled in her driveway.

"What are these? Oh, LuAnne, we wrote checks for these bills last week, remember? These should have been in the mail days ago."

She just looked at me and blinked.

To her, I added, "Don't worry about it. It's my fault. I should have mailed them the day we wrote the checks. It's okay."

To myself, I said, "Why haven't you made all her bills direct deposit? Why do you make things so difficult?"

I followed as she walked to her bedroom and sat on the edge of the bed. I knelt and took her shoes off, gently, one by one, and as I placed the second shoe on the floor, a text came through on my phone creating a noise that seemed to confuse LuAnne. Wes's words read, "Need a break from packing? Meet me at the shooting range? It's been far too long." LuAnne watched with wonder as I typed on the tiny keypad. "No time for a break. Maybe next time." A more honest reply would have been, "The last time I touched my gun was three months ago, and our lives had been in upheaval ever since. The thought of standing next to you firing at paper targets makes me feel sick." What Wes didn't know, couldn't know, was that I wouldn't see a paper target in front of me, I would see my brother.

I tossed my phone on the carpet next to LuAnne's shoes and watched as she stretched out on the bed. Without pulling back the covers, she patted the space beside her.

"Do you ever feel guilty?" she asked as I stretched out, the two of us facing one another.

"About what?"

"Being alive."

"Every day," I said this without hesitation, and she, without hesitation, closed her eyes. I watched her for several minutes, noting the lines on her face that had slowly come over the years. I wanted, no matter what was to come, to remember her face. As my own eyes began to blur and blink heavily, her face became distorted. Through the twisted lens, I thought I saw my mother's face before me, and because time doesn't exist when you're sleeping, I have no idea how long I was out before I heard a voice that, for an instant, I mistook as my mother's.

"Wake up. Hey, wake up."

As my eyes darted open, I whispered, "Gidget."

LuAnne peered at me with drowsy eyes. "Your cellular device is ringing."

It was Sadie. I was late picking them up. I instructed Sadie to walk to the elementary school and wait with Finn. By the tone of her voice, you would have thought she had been asked to stand on the corner holding a sign that read, "I'm a loser, please stare and ridicule me while you're passing by" with her little brother standing next to her sucking his thumb and wearing a unicorn costume.

"I'm so sorry," I pleaded as they both climbed into the car. I glanced in the rearview mirror and realized I had lines on my face from LuAnne's pillow. Sadie let out a deep sigh and shook her head.

"What?" I asked.

"What? You forgot us."

"I didn't forget you. I was with your grandmother, and I fell asleep."

"Oh, that's responsible," she snapped, her voice growing louder with every word.

"Sadie . . ."

"And don't say being normal is hard," she interrupted. "This isn't about being normal, it's about being responsible. You're supposed to be helping

Grandma pack, not be sleeping. I mean, have you seen your face? You look ridiculous."

"Sadie," I said sharply.

"Faith," she retorted, deflating every cell in my body. In that one moment, with those five letters, I had been demoted.

"That's funny." Finn chimed in, "I forgot your name is Faith. You know, 'cause to me your name is Mom. Can I call you Faith too?"

"No, Finn," Sadie said in retaliation for all the wrongs in the world, "She *is* your mom. So you should call her that."

I glared at Sadie with narrowed eyes. This was more than a demotion; she was waging war. I was prepared for this battle; I saw it coming, and I had been waiting in the trenches, waiting for the words that needed to be spoken—kind words, harsh words, words that would keep us both up at night. But I hadn't considered Finn. I wasn't willing for him to be caught in the crossfire. So I would surrender instead because, often, tomorrow's freedom is today's surrender. I would lose all credibility with my daughter, and my son would never know the bullet I took for him that day, but I was okay with that. We would drive home in silence. We would drive home with a wall so thick between us that I imagined my car dragging on the ground from the extra weight.

At the house, Sadie moved from the car to her room with her head held high. I went from the car to the kitchen like a wounded dog with my tail between my legs.

"Mom, this came for you." Finn held up a large manila envelope, and a shiver shot up my spine. "It says David Monroe PI. Is that a PI like a private investigator?"

"It is." I squeezed my shoulder blades together and rolled my head from side to side.

"Can I open it?"

I snatched it from his hand before answering, "It's my mail, thank you."

"Why are you communicating with a private investigator? Are you leading a double life? You *are* leading a double life, aren't you? I've always told Sadie you're not boring."

I hid my face, momentarily, with the envelope then explained, "This is research for a book I've been asked to write."

He stood, examining me. "You're still not boring. I think you're cool."

"Thanks."

"Oh, what about my experiment? Did you put the mold in Grandma's coffee?" His face was lit up like a Christmas tree.

"No, I didn't." His entire demeanor changed: his shoulders slumped, his cheeks fell. I had unplugged the Christmas tree and the lights had gone out.

"I'm sorry, Finn. We didn't have coffee today. We had ice cream. I guess I could have told her they were sprinkles, but I think dissolving it in coffee is a better way to go. I'm waiting for the right opportunity."

"Okay," he said, after considering the situation. "But maybe it's worth trying both. You know, hot and cold. I hadn't considered the difference between a hot and cold delivery method."

Finn stood, biting his bottom lip, lost in thought. I stood watching him, in awe of his curiosity and intellect. I made a mental note to buy him a child-sized lab coat. He could be a mad scientist for Halloween.

"Don't worry," I assured him. "I'll find the perfect time and the perfect delivery method." We exchanged winks, and while Finn bounded up the stairs to his room, I turned the envelope over in my hands, chuckling at the thought of me leading a double life. He wasn't wrong, actually. I placed the envelope on the countertop in front of me, and we stared at one another for several minutes until I slid it down into my purse where it still seemed to whisper, taunting me. I moved my purse to its usual spot by the front door then moved about the house picking up dirty laundry, using random socks and shirt sleeves to wipe up dust as I went from room to room. I had just closed the lid on the washing machine when I heard that envelope, all the way from downstairs, calling. My heartbeat sped up, and my face felt flush. As I left the laundry room, my fingers landed on the light switch and froze. I turned the light off and stood holding my breath, fighting the urge to turn it back on again. The call was there, in my face, in my head, swimming in the air around me. It had streamed up the stairs like the smell of freshly brewed coffee in the morning. Its voice was all too familiar, and I couldn't stand it. I smacked my palm against the light switch and took off in a sprint.

As I passed Finn's bedroom I heard, "Mom, are you okay?" I didn't answer but flew down the stairs where I grabbed the envelope from my purse, opened the front door, and found myself outside looking from side to side. I needed what was inside the envelope, but I wasn't ready to face it. Not yet. I opened the passenger door to my car and flung it on the seat. I was back at the front door of the house before I ran, once again, to the car and stuffed the envelope under the passenger seat. I didn't want it greeting me first thing the following morning. As I closed the car door, through the window, I saw LuAnne's overdue bills sticking out from the center console. I pressed my forehead against the window, acutely aware that I did very little right, and then wiped the grease mark away with my sleeve before slinking back to the house.

Most days I desperately wanted the day I was in to be over, yet I met the new mornings with dread, as I knew, at least for the foreseeable future, it would be just as daunting. Tomorrow always bore the stain of today; just like the crusty white spot I would find on my shirt that evening from the vanilla ice cream I had with LuAnne. I noticed the white spot as I set the dinner table that evening and realized, as if seeing them for the first time, that our dishes and serving bowls were also solid white. Each plate that slid from my hand onto the table took me one step deeper into my memories, memories I hated revisiting but couldn't refuse.

I could have been five years old; I could have been eleven or even fifteen: I was back in my mother's kitchen, setting out the blue and yellow patterned plates and silverware, my brother grabbing the matching serving bowls full of food.

"There's going to be a surprise at dinner," my brother said to me with a smirk. "I found some hornet spray and mouse poison in the garage." He raised his eyebrows and looked down at our dinner. I instantly began to sweat, then and now.

He continued to taunt me, "Don't worry about me. I know what not to eat. But the rest of you, well, we'll just see how the rest of you feel after dinner."

"Hon, are you alright?" Wes put his hand on my back. I marveled at the fact that I didn't even notice him or the kids sit down for dinner.

"I'm fine. I'll be right back, go ahead and fill your plates."

I went to the bathroom and stared at myself in the mirror; then closed my eyes when I got tired of my own face. I ran my hands under the cold water and then patted the coolness up my arms and on my neck. I pulled at my shirt sleeves as I walked back to the table

"Where's Sadie?"

"She asked if she could eat in her room."

"And you told her yes?"

Wes looked at me and half nodded his head.

"Can I eat in my room?" Finn asked excitedly.

Wes leaned back in his chair and rubbed his hand over his face, "Sure, buddy. You can eat in your room too."

Finn picked up his plate then set it back down. "Nah, I'd rather eat with you guys."

Wes glanced at me and winked. I glanced at Finn, who winked at me too.

I gave Finn an exaggerated wink and asked, "How's your book?"

"It's riveting," he answered, examining his dinner.

"I don't remember, how did the boys get separated from their parents?"

"You don't remember because I didn't tell you. They were in buses on a safari tour, and then there was an elephant stampede. Their bus was knocked over, and everyone started freaking out and running. Some people got crushed by the elephants, but don't worry, the description wasn't too graphic. Anyway, the two boys ran and managed to hide behind some boulders. But then . . ."

I have no idea what else Finn said about the book. He lost me at boulders. I thought about how I wouldn't mind finding some boulders to hide behind. I wanted to hide; with desperation, I wanted to hide, but the voice inside told me to keep running, run with the stampede as if it were a race. I pictured myself running, and I wondered how long the race was. Wes had a 26.2 sticker on the bumper of our car. If I had my own sticker it would say, "I'll let you know when it's over."

"Could I have a pocket knife?" I heard Finn ask.

"I'm sorry, what?"

He raised one side of his mouth and eyebrow, "You're inattentive. You're inattentive a lot these days."

I opened my mouth, then closed it. Wes snickered then cleared his throat.

"Could I have a pocket knife?" he asked again.

"No," I answered, my hand instinctively, protectively spreading over my right shoulder.

Later, in private, Wes would remind me that Finn is not my brother. But for now, he would simply lock eyes with me from across the table with a look of annoyance, but also with empathy because he knew what there was to know about me.

"If I pout and mope around and raise my voice occasionally can I have a pocket knife?"

"Finn . . ."

"Well," he put his elbows on the table and opened his hands towards the ceiling, "That's what Sadie's been doing, and it seems to be working for her."

"Okay," Wes said, "Let's start this conversation over. Tell us why you want a pocket knife."

"Arthur has one, and it's practical. It's a must-have in any survival situation."

"Who's Arthur?"

"Mom, he's one of the boys of Botswana. He has a pocket knife, and so he carves his initials and an arrow on trees and stumps so that if anyone's looking for them, they can follow their trail."

"Smart," Wes said with a quick nod.

"I don't want you carving our trees." I snapped. Then to apologize for snapping I added, "unless you're lost in the backyard, then, of course, you can carve the trees so I can find you."

"Mom, our backyard is the size of our house. If I get lost back there, you need to have my head examined."

This—the idea of getting his head examined—made me think of LuAnne and the havoc her disease was causing in her brain. This, of course, made me think about Wes and wonder if this would also be his fate. I wouldn't allow myself to question such things about Finn. I watched Wes from across the dinner table talking with Finn about pocket knives, survival, and Africa. Finn would like to go there one day, he said, get semi-lost and use his pocket knife to survive. Wes asked if he could please get semi-lost a little closer to home. These, I was starting to realize, were the important conversations. The nonsensical, never gonna happen conversations. It's in the nonsensical, in the dreaming together, where relationships are born. This is how we learn to talk, to really talk to each other. But what was it all for? Why build relationships if one day they would all be erased from your memory?

Before Vernon died, he took my hand and made me promise to look after his wife. Something he knew I would do without him asking, but he asked all the same. He had put aside some money, he told me, and I was to take LuAnne on a trip, just the two of us, just as soon as she was able to travel after his burial. I was to take her anywhere she wanted to go. "Make new memories," he said. Then, with teary eyes, he added, "As adults, we don't always remember the author or plot of every book we read as children. But we do know the books shaped us, and we carry those stories with us, as part of who we are, even though we don't really remember them. Do you understand what I'm saying? Every experience my sweetheart has will shape her, and she'll carry it with her, even if she can't remember it later."

When LuAnne and I made plans to travel to Kentucky I assured her that Vernon had something more in mind—somewhere tropical, perhaps—but she wanted to revisit the past while it still made itself available to her. Kentucky is where she and Vernon had honeymooned, and that is where she wanted to go.

"It changed," she said. "It's changed so much." It was by chance that we walked past Walton's Estate Jewelry, where Vernon had bought the pearls she had worn for over sixty years. The sign was still hanging in its place, but the lights were off, and there was a "For Lease" sign in the window. It had all changed so much. It was during our time in Kentucky that LuAnne tried butterscotch ice cream for the first time—a detail she didn't remember now, but a detail that proves Vernon was right. And, I suppose, that is what it's all about.

That night, I passed by Sadie's bedroom and said goodnight through her door; she didn't respond. Finn was fast asleep and didn't stir when I sat on his bed, played with his hair, and kissed his forehead, lingering over him. He smelled like a boy, and it made me smile; maybe the most sincere smile I had had all day. As I left his room, I ran my fingers along his spelling bee trophies and over the stacks of dictionaries and thesauruses that cluttered his desk. I made another mental note that everything, absolutely everything, needed dusting. My eyes were burning, my limbs hung heavy, and my bones felt dry. I crawled into bed and cuddled up next to Wes, and I realized that lying next to him was like finding a large shade tree in the middle of a scorching hot day. I allowed him to refresh me, and then, as he drifted into sleep, I crawled back out of bed unable to rest knowing those overdue bills were waiting in the car. The way my days were going, if it didn't happen now while no one else was needing my attention, it might never happen.

I slid in the driver's seat with my purse on my lap, the baggie of mold still sticking out and that dreaded envelope still imprisoned under the passenger seat. I pulled the baggie of mold out of my purse and shoved it in the console with the mail. There was a public trash can outside the post office; I could kill two birds with one stone. I would lie, I decided. I would lie to Finn about the mold. I would tell him I misplaced it. Or maybe that I put it in LuAnne's coffee, and it had no effect. I would think of something. I drove with the radio off, the windows down, and my arm sticking out the window. The air was chilly and made my skin prickle. Driving at night was something I enjoyed and wished for opportunities to do more. I could, I supposed, sneak out every night after Wes went to sleep. I wrinkled my face and pondered this possibility.

At the post office, I sat, staring at the rounded blue box. If LuAnne had been with me, she would have asked me to put in one envelope at a time, close the lid, and then open it again to make sure the mail went wherever it was supposed to go. If Finn had been with me, he would have asked me to put them down the shoot in alphabetical order, specifically based on the state where they were headed. Sometimes he wanted them sent by numerical order based on the zip code. It depended on his mood. But, LuAnne wasn't with me. Finn wasn't with me. No one was with me. I could put the mail in the slot however I wanted. I grabbed the stack, pulled the lid down, and away they went. All together and all at once. And that's when I realized it. I had dropped the baggie of mold down the neck of this rounded blue box along with a thin stack of non-alphabetized, overdue bills.

"It's okay," I said to myself. "I was going to throw it away anyway." I started to drive away but was stopped by an image of the mail carrier pulling out the baggie and thinking it was an act of terrorism. I could see it now, the front page of our local paper covered in pictures of people in hazmat suits surrounding the post office. I frantically started digging through my purse for a scrap of paper. There was a pen, but no paper. "I have two kids, how can I not have paper? Bingo!" I exclaimed, pulling out a wadded-up napkin from Twisty Freeze. After spreading out the napkin and rubbing my hand over and over it, trying to iron out the wrinkles with my sweat, I wrote in large letters, "SO SORRY ABOUT THE BAGGIE OF MOLD. I PROMISE IT'S NOTHING TOXIC LIKE ANTHRAX. IT'S A SCIENCE EXPERIMENT. I DROPPED IT DOWN THE SHOOT BY ACCIDENT."

I pulled down the metal flap and slid the note down into the deep. "Faith! You forgot to sign your name!" I plopped my head against the steering wheel causing a short beep from the horn. I didn't need to sign my name, did I? I mean, likely there were cameras on me anyway. Or, they'd test the paper for traces of DNA. They'd know it was from me within the next twenty-four hours. But, signing my name would save them time and resources. "I should have signed my name." I emptied my purse out on the passenger's seat; there were no more napkins. I looked around the post office and didn't see any cameras. And this wasn't TV, I reminded myself. They'll read the note and just have a good laugh. Right? They won't collect DNA. "Go home, Faith," said the voice inside, "Just go home." I could then see the follow up story, "Woman guilty of tainting postal box is the same woman who sent store-bought cookies for snack time."

I rolled up the window and slid down in my seat as far as possible to still be able to see over the steering wheel. I drove home with hot cheeks, a racing heart, and a promise to myself that I would never sneak out and drive at night again. Ever. I snuck back in the house, thankful that Wes was such a deep sleeper. I started to make my way back up the stairs but stopped myself. My mind was too active to sleep. I stayed downstairs where I would spend the next few hours folding laundry, watching *Little Women*, resurrecting memories, and secretly wishing I had a bag of Oreos to munch on.

The Lie

On our tenth anniversary, Wes and I went on a cruise to the Bahamas; we needed to escape the deafening silence in our house. On the second day, we befriended a couple while lounging next to the pool. The wife, whose name I can't recall after all these years, told me quickly that they had four children. One day, only a few weeks before, she had cried to her husband that if she had to make one more pot of mac and cheese or one more pitcher of Kool-Aid, she would kill herself. That same night, after putting the kids to bed, she and her husband decided to take this cruise. The husband, Lonny, asked us if we were also aboard this grand ship to escape the chaos of parenthood. I looked at Wes, telling him with my eyes that I would give my right arm to have children to make mac and cheese for and that I doubted making Kool-Aid took much energy.

Wes took my hand and said, "We're not in the mac and cheese stage. In fact, this is our honeymoon, so we're not thinking along those lines just yet." Wes squeezed my hand, and I squeezed his back.

She, Lonny's wife, congratulated us on our marriage and asked how many kids we wanted in the future. Before either of us could answer, she explained that she and Lonny were both from large families, and so naturally they wanted the same; they planned to have at least three more. In fact, they hoped to conceive on this very cruise; information that made me roll my eyes and fight back tears. Wes just squeezed my hand again. Did we come from large families, too? Lonny wanted to know. Wes said without hesitation that he was an only child. Then they all three looked at me. I'm also an only child, I told them. Lonny and his wife both let out a disapproving "oh," and Wes winked at me in a way that made me blush.

All four of us understood that we had very little, if anything, in common, and we would not be spending time together for the remainder of the cruise. I wasn't bothered by that, and I doubt Lonny and his wife were either. It was a good thing, to be honest, not spending more time with them. It would have been difficult to hide how well Wes and I knew each other after ten years of marriage. Reverting to the awkward honeymoon stage would have taken the relaxation out of our getaway. A facade that might have been entertaining in the beginning but would prove to be exhausting.

Over the years I've imagined us running into Lonny and his wife and me seeming inappropriate for remembering his name and not hers. I would confess that when we met, Wes and I were celebrating our tenth anniversary, not our honeymoon, and that we were escaping the reality of infertility. They would exchange glances and confess that they too were struggling with infertility. The four children, mac and cheese, and Kool-Aid was their version of a comfort-seeking lie. We would hug and apologize for not being honest and for not exchanging information and staying in touch; because we did, after all, have something in common. This daydream always ended with a deep sigh.

What I remember most about that trip was that Wes and I both told lies. We told them for ourselves and each other. On that trip, we weren't struggling with infertility, and I wasn't my brother's sister. I realize now, after all these years, that lying wasn't the answer. I know now that not being forthright with the truth leaves a dirty film on everything, like in spring when the farmers are preparing the fields, and everything gets covered with a layer of dust. The lie saturates the conscience and, in the long run, only makes the reality harder to bear. Like all pleasures in this life, the benefit of the lie is brief; momentary. For one week we lied, and let go of the two things that caused us the most pain. Though we never spoke to Lonny and his wife again, we continued to lie to ourselves; for one week. I loved Wes for lying on my behalf and for letting me lie. I loved him then, and I love him still—for this. But, the respite we found in that one week didn't erase the empty house we would come home to or prevent my brother from causing unrest in our lives, even after his death. As they say, the truth will out.

3

Wednesday

I sat across from my brother hoping no one would mistake us for a couple. It was enough to be seen with him in public, but to be mistaken for one of his many women made me feel sick inside. The restaurant was dimly lit, and there was soft piano music in the background. He had invited me to one of the many restaurants he owned, an intentional choice as he would be recognized, something he loved. Men nodded at him as they made eye contact; women either looked away quickly or smiled at him while touching their face or neck.

"Thanks for meeting me," he said in an almost whisper. "I apologize for not inviting Wesley, but I thought this conversation might be easier kept between the two of us, for now."

"What is it?"

"It has to do with Sadie."

"Mom." Finn stood before me, blinking excessively. I made a mental note; his hair won't cut itself. "Mom, you must dream deep too. I've been trying to wake you. I have this place I have to go to every day at the same time." He raised his eyebrows, "School."

"I'm sorry, I didn't hear my alarm."

"You heard it," he said. "You turned it off like two hours ago."

"Then why didn't you wake me two hours ago?"

"You're the parent. It's not my job to wake you."

"Well said." I pulled the covers over my head. I had become a terrible mother.

Moments later I crawled out of bed, my hands instinctively going to my temples, pressing and rubbing. I would find, as I made my way around the house that morning, that we were out of painkillers. I would drink extra coffee and hope for the best.

In the car, Finn nudged the back of my seat with his foot. "Mom, are you alright? You're sort of jittery."

"If you look up the word *jittery* in the dictionary," I answered, "there's a picture of me and like ten cups of coffee."

"If you looked up the word *cantankerous*, you'd see a picture of Sadie."

"Shut up," said Sadie.

"Okay. Okay," I said, in that irritating mom voice.

"Oh, wait. You'll like this one Sadie: if you looked up the word *lovebird*, you'd see a picture of you and Kyle."

"Finn, shut up!"

"Hey," I pointed at her with my mom finger, "PMS isn't an excuse to be mean."

"PMS," Finn chuckled. "If you looked that up you'd see—"

"Finn!" Sadie and I snapped in unison.

I hated to say it, but I was relieved to have both kids out of my car and under someone else's supervision for the next eight hours. Before going to LuAnne's, I had to make a stop at the pharmacy and pick up her prescription, something I had been doing for some time now at Wes's persistence. "I don't want to worry that she didn't get them," he would say. "Just because she has them doesn't mean she'll take them," I would reply. He would grimace and change the subject.

As I pulled open the pharmacy door Tiffany Ledbetter, whose husband was also on the police force, walked toward me, exiting the store. "Faith! How are you?" She hugged me, but not a typical hug with a quick pat on the back; she enveloped me with a strong, warm, intentional embrace. I thought for a moment, as I always did with her hugs, that I might fall asleep in her arms.

"Really," she released me but held on to both my hands. "I know you're moving LuAnne this week. Really, how are you?"

How was I? Instantly my face wrinkled, and she became a blurry blob.

"Oh, Faith." She squeezed my hands before letting them go. "You clearly need to talk, really talk." She looked at her wrist where there was no watch. "I have to be somewhere in like five minutes. Maybe one day next week we can get together and have coffee. Would that work for you?"

Would that work for me? I swiped at my cheeks and cleared my throat; I stood up a little taller and managed to say, "Yeah, thanks."

She smiled and promised to call next week; I smiled and promised myself that if she did call, I wouldn't answer. I watched her walk away; a piece of my heart stuck to the bottom of her shoe like a piece of gum.

Over the years Wes has teased me about not having many friends—real friends. He would say it's because I'm an author, and we prefer to be sad and left alone in dark corners. I would correct him and say it's because all the women in this town are troublemakers, and no one wants to hang out with the police chief's wife. But the truth is, I've never been good at being friends. As a child, I wanted close friends, but close friends invite each other to their houses and have sleepovers. It felt safer to keep my friends at a distance, away from the nightmare that slept in the next room. As an adult, I tried to let certain ladies get closer, let them in, but I found that most women, like Tiffany, didn't have time for the full package. They only had time for the outer layer, and I wasn't satisfied with that. The only female in my life that longed for the deeper things was wasting away, slowly ascending to the surface, struggling to navigate the deep. That is how I felt too. That and, despite the abundance of coffee, I still had a headache.

I grabbed a bottle of Advil on my way to the back of the store, opened it, dry swallowed three of them, then took my place next to the sign that read, "To protect the privacy of our patients, please wait behind the orange line." I tried not listening to the lady in front of me as she leaned over the counter talking to the pharmacist about her cocktail of antidepressants. If they really wanted to protect the privacy of their patrons, the thick orange line would be at least two isles back. Instead, the thick orange line was perfectly located for me to hear, even though I tried not to listen, that her husband was frustrated by her low libido.

I once wrote an entire novel based on a conversation I overheard between an elderly man and woman in line at this very pharmacy. Wes still teases me for making money off of eavesdropping, but it simply isn't my fault that the orange line is within earshot and that elderly people often think they're whispering when they're not. It's because of that novel's great success that I can't help but overhear, even though I try hard not to listen.

The woman with the low libido finally turned to walk away and shook her baggie of pills, as if she would know by the rattle whether they were all there or not. She looked down as she passed me rather than making eye contact.

"Next. Oh, Mrs. Moore. You need LuAnne's meds?"

Abby, the pharmacist's assistant who looks about twelve years old, turned and started flipping through the baggies without me answering. Then, after scanning the label she nodded at the bottle of Advil in my hand and asked, "Can I get you anything else?"

"Oh, yes. I opened this already. Sorry."

"Something hurt?"

"My head." I smiled a half smile and then examining the bottle said, "How much of this would stop my heart?"

"Excuse me?"

"Oh, nothing." I thought I had said that last part in my head.

"I heard what you said." Abby looked at me with wide eyes.

"Sorry, I just meant, my heart hurts too."

"Um, your heart hurts like you need to see a cardiologist?"

My half smile became a three-quarter smile. "No, no, I don't need to see a cardiologist. I just meant my heart hurts like I'm sad."

"I don't think any amount of Advil will take away . . . sad. Mrs. Moore, if you need to talk to someone, I can get the pharmacist."

"Oh, no. Thank you."

"Can I at least give you this?" She handed me a card with a number for a suicide hotline.

"Oh, I don't need that, but thank you." I placed the card on the counter and slid it across to her. She picked it up slowly and dropped it down in the bag with LuAnne's prescription. I was starting to sweat and involuntarily wiped at my forehead.

"I'm not . . . I was just . . ." And then I said what I always say when trying to lessen the awkwardness of my mere existence, "I'm a writer. And, you know . . . writers just say things. I promise I'm not suicidal. I was just thinking out loud, you know if I were writing about someone who was sad and their heart ached . . ."

We stood there for a moment just staring at one another.

"You said *you* were sad and that *your* heart aches." She slid her hand under the counter the way bank tellers do in the movies when they're pushing a silent alarm. The thought quickly crossed my mind that Abby and I should be friends—she was an excellent listener.

"I mean, I only took three Advil," I said, trying to smile a full smile.

"The recommended dose is one," she said, scanning the barcode.

"Right. Well, I didn't take the whole bottle. That says something, right?"

She didn't respond. I swiped my card, signed my name, grabbed the bag and walked away with my head down. I avoided making eye contact with the next person waiting behind the orange line.

I slid behind the wheel, started the engine, and as I clicked the seat belt in place, my cell phone rang, it was Wes.

"Hey, where are you?"

"Just leaving the pharmacy. Is something wrong?"

"No, I just . . . wanted to hear your voice."

I couldn't help but laugh, "Whatever. You're checking in on me. You were afraid I'd forget your mom's meds."

He didn't say anything, but I could hear him smiling.

"Your mom's the one with Alzheimer's, not me."

"I know. You've got a lot on your plate, I just wanted to make sure you remembered. And, for the record, I also wanted to hear your voice."

"Well, I remembered. And, hey . . . if someone calls you from the pharmacy . . . I promise it was a misunderstanding."

"Oh man, were you writing out loud again?"

"Something like that."

"What am I going to do with you?"

"Well, once we get your mom settled, it might be in everyone's best interest if I never left the house. Or at the very least, make sure I never interact with anyone . . . that would probably be a good idea."

"I love you," he said firmly.

I didn't say anything, but I knew he could hear me smiling.

"Faith," he took a deep breath, "I need you to hang in there, okay? We'll get through this."

"I know." And I did know. As exhausted as I was, somehow we would get through this. What bothered me though, was knowing we'd look different on the other side. I tossed my phone and LuAnne's meds on the passenger seat and felt a sudden surge of anxiety run through my body when I remembered the envelope exiled underneath the seat. I turned up the radio as a distraction and drove.

LuAnne was standing in the kitchen when I arrived at her house; her arms folded over her chest. She watched me set her medicine bottles in the center of her kitchen table. Once again I thought, just because she has them, doesn't mean she'll take them.

"I think we should tackle the kitchen today," she finally said with determination. "Everything but the coffee maker, that can go last. But, the dishes, pots and pans, all that can be boxed up today."

"You still have to eat," I reminded her.

"Well, you know, I don't really cook anymore. I have all those wonderful little trays in the freezer that have food on them."

"TV dinners?"

"Yes, yes. But, why do they call them that? I don't eat them in front of the television. Anyway, the girls in my card club are taking me out tonight; one last hurrah—"

"One last hurrah?" I interrupted.

"Well," She ran her fingers over her pearls. "I think I read somewhere that there's a curfew at River Side. So, this is one last hurrah while I'm still my own boss. You understand. Then I thought maybe I could invite myself to dinner at your house tomorrow night. Then by dinner time on Friday, I'll be in my new home." She raised her eyebrows, "What do you think?"

"I think you've got it all figured out."

"Then let's have it." She wiped her hands on her pants as if she'd already put in a day's work.

The kitchen, in my opinion, is the heart of the home. All the other rooms are connected by veins with the kitchen pumping life into them. With each room we packed up, I felt a bit like we had performed an amputation, taking an arm or a leg, but as a whole, the body would survive. The kitchen, however, would prove most difficult, as we would be detaching the heart. As we moved around the room, memories passed before us like photographs, the past peeking from behind corners and popping out from drawers and cupboards. The ghosts of who we once were lingered in the room, peering over our shoulders, daring us to remember. There were echoes of laughter that turned to cackles and snorts and tears that, if collected over the years, would flood the entire house. LuAnne would stand, frozen in concentration, grasping at the details of memories, the way we do when a word sticks to the tip of our tongue but just won't let go. As LuAnne strained, holding tight to what would soon be lost, I saw a woman made of braided rope, the rope unraveling. I saw myself grasping; one hand over the other as quickly as I could trying to get my grip on the braid and keep it intact. But the unraveling was always one step ahead, proving unstoppable. I could only watch the threads separate, her being reshaped, repurposed. Though her outward appearance wasn't changing, I feared she would soon be unrecognizable.

My heart skipped a beat, causing me to gasp for breath. LuAnne looked at me with wide eyes, "Are you okay, dear?"

I managed a quick, squeaky, "I'm fine." But I wasn't. I thought perhaps I was dying. Was it possible to die from guilt? It did, after all, manifest itself like a disease with its physical demands and bending of the mind. Guilt, I had decided, was a slow, agonizing, life-sucking disease. My heart skipped again, and I coughed after drawing in a stunted breath. LuAnne glared at me and put her hands on her hips as if to scold me.

"I'm okay, really." I forced a smile. "I'm just going to use the bathroom."

I let the cold water run over my hands for several minutes, something I did as a child that always brought an odd sense of comfort. Then I sat on the toilet and let out a sigh. Moments later I sighed again as I realized there was no toilet paper. I looked over my shoulder to the basket sitting on the tank, empty. I looked on the floor around me, nothing. I couldn't help but chuckle to myself, and for a moment I looked forward to telling Sadie about this. We would laugh together, and she would nudge me and tell me I'm awesome. This would be the start of a new inside joke, a joke we would call "the drip dry." While I enjoyed that image of us laughing together, I knew deep down I wouldn't tell her about this. A few months ago she would have laughed; now she would roll her eyes and think I was stupid. And, she would be right—I was stupid. Not just for this, but for many, many things. Things she doesn't even know about, things that will haunt me the rest of my days. Things that the voice inside tells me to let go of, but I haven't found the nerve. I had become comfortable in my stupidity. It was familiar. And the realization of that made me feel really, really stupid.

I stood, pulled up my pants, and felt the uncomfortable wetness. I sighed again, then opened LuAnn's medicine cabinet in hopes of finding a stray roll of toilet paper or at least a box of Kleenex. Instead, I found bottles and bottles of pain relievers, sleeping pills, chemo pills; you name it, she had it. I shook my head and grabbed the basket from the tank and filled it to the brim with medicine bottles. They all had Vernon's name on them and held memories that brought tears to my eyes. More uncomfortable wetness.

LuAnne was walking past the bathroom when I opened the door. She looked down at the basket in my hands and gasped. "Why do you have those?" She took them from my hands in one fell swoop. "I'm not ready to get rid of these," she said, cradling the basket. For a moment, she was childlike, but only for a moment. "I know this must seem silly to you," she said in a low voice, "but these medicines hold so many memories for me. And not just sad memories, you see. Vernon and I had such good conversation during those last weeks, me as his nurse. I'll take care of these, I promise. Soon."

"I was just trying to help."

"I know that. I know that." She set the basket on a stack of boxes and smiled saying, "Let's go see Vernon. It's been a few days since my last visit. Would you mind driving me there?" She raised her eyebrows and grinned with such innocence. I realized as I smiled back at her that I had been wrong. The kitchen might be the heart of the home, but it wasn't the heart of our family. She was. As long as she was with us, the blood would still flow.

At the cemetery, we stood, hand in hand, before my father-in-law's headstone.

"It's been two years today since Vernon left us." She squeezed my hand as she spoke.

"Oh, LuAnne. I'm sorry, I didn't realize . . ."

"Don't apologize," she said sweetly. "He was my love, not yours. This is for me to remember, not you."

"Two years," I said in amazement while wanting to say, "It's actually been three."

"Two years too long," she said under her breath. At that, she let go of my hand and started to sit.

"LuAnne," I said, grabbing her arm. "You don't need to sit on the ground."

She stood up straight, pushed her shoulders back, looked me square in the eye and said, "It's my mind that's broken, not my body."

I let go of her arm and took a step back. She sat herself down in front of Vernon's headstone and patted the ground next to her. I heard my knees crackle as I bent to sit down.

"I don't want to forget him," she said in an almost whisper. Then in her normal voice, "You know, right before Vernon died, he told me that he hated to leave me just yet, but he knew I would be okay." She leaned into me and rubbed against my shoulder. "He said he knew I'd be okay because he knew that you would take good care of me."

"It's my privilege to take care of you."

"Ah, it's also your duty. I think there's a law or something that says you have no choice." She glanced at me quickly and chuckled. "I'd like to be alone with Vernon, if you don't mind."

"LuAnne, I can't leave you."

"I didn't say anything about leaving me." She made a shooing motion with her hands, "Go visit your parents. You can keep an eye on me from there."

I let out a deep sigh. LuAnne took my hands in hers and kissed them, holding them to her lips for several seconds. "I shared a bed with this man for many years. I'd like to sleep with him again. Would that be okay with you?" Then she added quickly, "I'd like to just lie here and take a little nap."

"LuAnne. I really don't think . . ." Before I could finish my sentence, she had stretched herself out over Vernon's plot. She tucked her hands under her head. "Just for a bit," she said with a grin on her face.

I looked around again. There were no other visitors. Why did this seem so strange? Yet, why did this also seem so sweet and appropriate? Who was I to tell a woman she couldn't take a nap on the grave of her dead husband?

"Just for a bit," I said sternly. As I stood to walk away, she called my name and said she loved me. I pretended I didn't hear her.

I walked six rows over and found my parents. Their flowers were faded. I hated silk flowers, but real ones seemed so frivolous. They couldn't see them, after all. I glanced at LuAnne. She was still there. Reluctantly, I sat before my parent's grave; their headstone etched with intertwining hearts. Their names were there, their birthdates, and death dates. September 11, 2001. I still shake my head at this, losing both parents on the same day, losing them in such a horrific, dumb, wasteful way.

My brother had offered our parents an opportunity that, he said, would set them up for life. He said the investment was a no-brainer. Easy money. They could enjoy a carefree retirement. My parents traveled to New York City to sign the papers. "He could overnight you the papers," I told my mom. "I've never been to New York," she said. So they went. They spent the first day sightseeing and had Italian food in a tiny little place with drippy candles. I know this because my mom sent a postcard and told me. She loved drippy candles. I loved that she sent a postcard when they were only going to be gone for three days. On the second day, they took a taxi to the World Trade Center. They sat in my brother's office for over an hour. Waiting. He was late. He was not there when the building fell. I hated him then, and I hate him now, for this.

I sat at my parent's grave, even though they weren't there. Their ashes were scattered about a city they had never been to before. A city that didn't know them. A city that wouldn't miss them. But, I had missed them for fourteen years. Every day. And every day I have hated my brother for taking them from me. I hated him for not overnighting the papers, for not being there with them so that they had to die surrounded by strangers, and I hated him for not being nice enough to blame himself for any of those things. I suppose if I'm being honest, I hated myself too. I had devoted countless hours of my life to flipping light switches and dabbling in other rituals that took time, time that I can't get back. And in the end, I couldn't keep them alive.

Hate, so I'm finding, is not like a rock that sits on the ground waiting to be kicked or stumbled over. Hate is more like a fancy weed that pushes its roots deep down and sprouts flowers on top to get your attention. Only you don't know that they're poisonous until you've picked them, brought them home, placed them on display, and broken out in a rash. My mom told me once, while I helped her weed the garden, that it wasn't enough to break the weed off at ground level; the roots had to be plucked out, or it would simply grow back. She also told me the best time to weed—getting roots and all—was right after a rainstorm, when the ground was good and soft from the soaking. I've wondered over the years if I cried enough, got myself good and wet, could I get my brother out of my heart, roots and all. I wondered this because to me it seemed that hate was more than a feeling; he was hate. I wasn't sure I could get rid of the emotion without getting rid of him. But now I know that even though he's dead, he isn't gone. I possess the best and worst parts of him; he's with me every day.

This hate made me think of my great Aunt Hazel; a woman who I never met but, from pictures, greatly resemble. Although my father didn't know the details of what drove his Aunt Hazel mad, he knew that she died of consumption. She was consumed by hate; this my father said with a smirk, as if it were the cleverest thing. Hazel never married and rarely left her home.

My father, because Hazel and his mother were sisters, went with his mother sometimes to visit her. There was one visit in particular my father told me about. Aunt Hazel had met him and his mother at the front door, keeping them in the foyer for some time with small talk. My father remembered letting go of his mother's hand and walking over to the couch. As he was sitting down, Hazel ran toward him, grabbed his arm, and pulled him away.

"You can't sit here without protection," she hissed. "There's no telling what you've brought in from the streets." Hazel then left the room and returned with a towel. She smoothed the towel out over the cushions of the couch, stood up straight, and simply said, "There."

"Her breath smelled awful," my father had told me. "It was like something deep inside of her was rotting."

My father recounted that he sat on that ratty, old towel for almost an hour while his mother and Aunt Hazel talked in the kitchen. He remembered spending that time looking around the room at all the knickknacks. He wasn't as interested in the collection of stuff as much as he was in the inches of dust that covered everything. He could hear the ladies talking, their voices quiet at first, but then becoming raised and harsh. He remembered hearing their high heeled shoes clip clopping on the linoleum floor and then the familiar sound of water coming from the kitchen sink. He stood and tiptoed across the room and into the kitchen. His Aunt Hazel was leaning against the sink drinking a tall glass of water.

"I'm thirsty," he said to his mother.

"Well, that's too bad," Aunt Hazel chuckled, "We're fresh out of water."

"Hazel, really?" My grandmother reached to open the cupboard, presumably to get my father a glass. Hazel grabbed her sister's arm and said in her rotting voice, "It's time for you and your street rat to go."

In the car, my grandmother, through her tears, explained to my father that Hazel had experienced something terrible, something so terrible that she just couldn't find her way out of the pain. "She was consumed by it," my grandmother had said. She was consumed, and it had changed her. Hazel had allowed the seed of bitterness to take root in her heart, and it had turned to hate. A deep and complex hate. A year later Hazel wrote her sister a letter saying that she just couldn't take it anymore; she hated everyone, most of all herself. Hazel wrote that she was most certainly losing her mind, that her emotions had gotten the better of her, and that she could no longer think of anything else, ever. Her life was nothing but one dark room after another, which took the joy out of living because all the rooms looked the same and were equally empty. She was tired of all the feelings, she had said; there were too many of them to feel at the same time. There were simply too many.

After Hazel mailed that letter, she admitted herself to a psychiatric hospital where she lived the remainder of her days heavily sedated. She died in her sleep, alone and angry. My father told me this not long before he and my mother went to New York. I've wondered many times if he shared this with me because he saw more than a physical resemblance between Hazel and myself. But it has made me wonder over the years what allowed me to not lose myself to all the feelings, to the hate. What kept me afloat and what caused her to sink? Did she reach a point, a crossroads, where she looked around and said, "Yes, I believe I'll dive headfirst into this pool of madness"? This is something I didn't understand because from my point of view, as skewed as it may be, I felt as though I had every right to lose my mind. But, how could I? I did marry. I did have children. I had LuAnne: people depended on me. There simply wasn't time to go mad. Going mad would be self-indulgent, and there simply wasn't time.

It was possible, I assumed, that going mad wasn't a choice, that there were no crossroads. I sometimes envisioned a bridge inside each of us, linking our minds and hearts. Maybe Aunt Hazel's bridge was the swinging type, and her too many feelings caused the bridge to swing so wildly that everything toppled over the side. Or, perhaps her bridge was perfectly steady, but the too-many-feelings jammed the bridge and, reaching its maximum capacity, caused a catastrophic crumble. Maybe, just maybe, the bridge was empty, but there was still too much noise, and the only way to make it stop was to jump. It occurred to me then that perhaps I was stronger than my great Aunt Hazel. Perhaps I was proof that it was possible to feel all the feelings and still not be overcome. It was also possible, I realized, that I had not yet felt all the feelings. This thought, I admit, terrified me.

The thought that there might be more to feel, more that might actually push me over the edge, stayed with me as I drove LuAnne back home from the cemetery for lunch. I thought about asking the pizza delivery guy, as I handed him money, if I looked terrified, if it was obvious. If I only knew what it was exactly that Aunt Hazel had been through, maybe then I could reconcile in my own mind that she was justified, that there was no other way out. Then I could compare her life with my own and find a just cause, a reason for staying sane. But then again, we can't compare lives or the tragedies we face. Comparison will only make the bridge more unstable and the leap off the side more wasteful.

Comparison is dangerous, yet it seems to be ingrained in our Western culture. Sadie had often confessed to me that she compares herself to the other girls at school. She wondered what it was that made some girls want to play sports while others wanted to stand on the sidelines and cheer the rest on. What made some girls feel at home at the end of a cigarette while she felt at home behind her cello or hovering over her sketch pad or swirling in her watercolors? She couldn't help but wonder what life would be like in the shoes of one of these other girls, how differently the boys would look at her if she wore makeup or had long blonde hair. And her body, she would say, don't get her started on that—the comparisons there would make my head spin. But Sadie never considered that I was young once too, and the comparison game wasn't new to her generation. She didn't invent comparison. She also didn't believe me when I told her the comparison game doesn't always end when you become an adult. She nudged me when I told her this and thanked me for trying to be relatable. One day, unfortunately, she would know I was relatable because I could, in fact, relate.

I longed to have those conversations with Sadie again. I missed her; like LuAnne, she had changed. I picked her up from school that day and endured, once again, her silence. Finn, as usual, had no trouble filling the empty air telling us all about his day.

"It was so lame," he said. "We had to tell the class about our parents and grandparents and where they were from, and then we colored in states on a big map to see how many states were represented by our class."

"Why was that lame? That sounds interesting."

"Because I was the only one that filled in just one state. O-H-I-O."

Sadie started rubbing her face, concentrating on her eyes with slow, deep circles.

"Well, my parents weren't originally from Ohio," I told him.

"Yes, they were. You were born here."

"I was born here, yes. But, my parents moved to Ohio from California."

"Californ-i-a? As in palm trees and movie stars?"

"The very one."

"They left Californ-i-a to come to O-H-I-O? Why would they do that?"

I chuckled, stealing a glance at Sadie who was now picking at her fingernails. I then realized how little I had told them about my parents. I suppose I wasn't the type to wear my loved ones on my sleeve. Instead, I folded them up and carried them in my pocket. Kept them for me.

"I'm not really sure," I said with a sigh.

"But, I mean, why Ohio? Did they have friends here? Why here?"

"My parents just always said they needed a change, so they moved. But, I'm glad they came here because I met your dad here."

From the corner of my eye, I saw Sadie shake her head and let out a deep breath.

"Was your brother born here or there?"

"There."

"What did your parents do again? You know, for work."

"My dad was an editor."

"Oh right, that's why I love words. I got that from him," Finn said.

"Yes." I smiled. "My mom was a school teacher in California, but she stopped teaching when they moved to Ohio. After I was old enough to start school, she started subbing."

"Like a substitute teacher?"

"Yep."

"Subs are the best. They let you watch movies instead of do school work. I bet she was a cool sub."

"I bet so."

And that was that. For Finn, the sum of my parent's existence was about loving words and being a cool sub. I thought perhaps I should take them out of my pocket more often, let Sadie and Finn see that there was more, so much more, to my parents than that.

As we pulled into the driveway, Finn expressed his excitement over telling his teacher the next day that he could now color in the state of Californ-i-a. I pictured his teacher rolling her eyes as he overemphasized the i-a. I dropped my purse by the door as usual and slipped off my shoes and followed Sadie across the room.

"Sadie, honey. You're bleeding through your pants," I whispered.

She quickly swiped her hand across her bottom and took a deep breath.

"I'm gonna go shower." She walked away tugging at her shirt trying to cover the spot.

After sorting through the mail, I picked up the laundry basket and followed her up the stairs. As I walked through the hallway, I could hear the water hitting the bathtub floor like rain. The slapping sound was almost violent; I stopped to listen and closed my eyes. After several seconds I turned my head, and when I opened my eyes, I saw that Sadie's bedroom door was open. I hadn't set foot in her room in far too long; an agreement Wes and I had made to give her something that was all her own, her own space, her own pit to crawl into. Setting the laundry basket at my feet, I stepped towards her door, looked back to the bathroom then, pushing my hair from my face, stepped over the invisible line and felt a surge of emotion as I pushed my toes into her carpet. Sadie had dropped her backpack just inside her door, I started to move it—an old habit—but that would only leave proof that I had crossed into forbidden territory; it would have to stay put. I had feared that her anger and discontent would bleed over into her room, but it hadn't. Her room was just as it always had been. Everything had a place, and everything was in its place. Her dresser and nightstand were lined with books, still organized in alphabetical order. The cello, in its hard shell, stood leaning in the corner. Her bed was made, and I couldn't help but run my fingers over the silky comforter; her childhood teddy bear still sitting at attention against her pillows.

I sat on the floor, my back against her bed, surveying the artwork that covered her walls, sketches brought to life with watercolor. There were photographs of her and Claire and her and Kyle taped to her mirror. On her chest of drawers, our family picture was lying face down. I smiled and felt a twinge of hope that we were simply face down and not in a drawer under her socks. This allowed me to relax a bit, and as I leaned into her bed, I felt a sharp point on my shoulder, turning around I found her journal sticking out, a fraction of an inch, from under the mattress. I reached for it without thinking and pulled it from its hiding place; it wasn't until I opened to the first page that what I was doing hit me. I was crossing every line, breaking every rule, ignoring every covenant between a parent and child. I peeked over the bed towards her door and could still hear the shower; she wouldn't know I was here or that I read her secret thoughts. I was doing her a favor, wasn't I? Wasn't it best to know what she was thinking right now? What if she was having thoughts of cutting herself, I heard that was a thing with girls her age. Wouldn't it be best for us all if I knew?

Running my fingers over her handwriting made me overly aware of the coldness of the page. Whatever warmth had lingered from her touch had long since disappeared. Flipping through the pages I began to read an entry from two weeks ago. I whispered her words aloud as I read them.

My pen a fountain
Black waters flow by anger's inspiration
Words spill off my fingertips
Splashing onto the tree
The tree
Put to death for the sake of my escape

She had firmly retraced the words anger, inspiration, death, and escape, making them stand out from the others. If I squinted my eyes the letters seemed to stretch and bend giving a deformed and unnatural movement to the words. I ran my fingers over her writing and then I heard it: the clunk of the pipes as she turned off the water. Words I would never say out loud ran through my mind as I twisted my body and pushed the journal back under the mattress. I jumped to my feet then bent back down; how far was the journal sticking out? Did I put it back in the same place? Did I disrupt the sheets? She would know, she would know I was here, and she would never trust me ever again. I deserved it, I told myself. Whatever came, I deserved it.

As I tugged on her comforter to smooth it out, I heard the squeaking of the bar rolling under her wet towel, and in the next second, I heard her bump the door as she pulled her housecoat from the hook. I was at the foot of her bed when I heard the doorknob rattle. With my eyes fixed on the door, I set off in a half jump half sprint, my foot catching the strap of her backpack. I stumbled with my arm flailing wildly; my knuckles nicked the door frame as I fell towards the floor face first, the laundry basket catching my fall as my ribs hit its rim. Moaning, I rolled off the laundry basket, and onto the floor in the fetal position.

"What are you doing?" Sadie stepped over me as she asked this. I couldn't answer, the pain in my side was too sharp. I wanted to grab her ankle and pull her down with me but I was too slow. She closed the door to her room without waiting for an answer or without checking to see if I was hurt. The thought crossed my mind that our family picture hadn't made it in a drawer yet because, to her, we weren't worth the energy it would take, not because she wanted to steal a glimpse of us every once in a while.

I laid there, for a moment, waiting to catch my breath but also to see if Sadie stormed back out of her room demanding to know why I invaded her privacy. When the storm didn't come I willed myself to my knees and, like a child, pushed the laundry basket down the hallway into my bedroom and crawled to the full-length, oval mirror standing in the corner, one of the few things I took from my parent's house after they died. I knelt before my reflection examining my ribs, finding it painful to simply lift my arm to get a good look. Bruises were already forming as were the excuses I would give Wes to justify my actions. But I knew in the end he would laugh at my audacity and marvel at my courage; he would kiss the bruises and whisper in my ear that he loved me.

I unzipped my jeans and opened the flap, exposing the silvery lines down the sides of my belly. Sadie had asked me once in a dressing room what those lines were. I explained that a woman's skin stretches when a baby grows inside, and after the baby comes out, the woman is left with these marks. It's like a mommy badge, I had told her. I realize now that she had every right to assume those marks had her name on them. She had every right to assume she had grown inside of me. Now I wished more than anything that I had told her these particular marks had Finn's name on them; that I had then ripped open my chest and showed her my heart. This, I would tell her, is where I keep your stretch marks.

These stretch marks, the ones on my heart, led me to labor over another memory. A part of me was deeply disturbed that my memories weren't coming in chronological order but I couldn't let that ruin the moment. When a memory came, I had to get it down, document it. I kept reminding myself that these writings weren't meant to be seen. This exercise was meant to bring forth the bits and pieces that would mesh together and form my brother's story. Whatever I wrote now, whatever memories came, were safe. This thought gave me the confidence to keep typing when Sadie appeared on the screen before me. She was safe; her story was safe. No one was going to see this. I chanted these words to myself as my fingers moved around the keyboard. Sadie had every right to hate me. She had every right to see Wes and me as untrustworthy. She had every. Single. Right. As the memory spewed out before me on the screen, I saw more, read more, between the lines. I saw every mistake I had ever made. Each regret, every shortcoming was there. My failures, not just as a mother but as a person, were overwhelming me; screaming inside my head. I felt paralyzed by my faults and how my faults, all ten zillion of them, had affected my daughter.

I didn't reread this memory. I couldn't. Instead, I stretched out on the bed and texted Wes, "Bring home pizza?" I deserved pizza twice in one day. I deserved the extra calories, the artery clogging cheese and greasy pepperoni. And, as an extra dose of punishment, I would assure extra weight settled on my hips by once again refusing to run with Wes.

"Pizza!" Finn exclaimed, "A giant round mess of awesomeness!"

Sadie took her seat without a word, slid a slice of awesomeness onto her plate.

"Guess what?"

In his authoritative dad voice, Wes said, "Don't talk with your mouth full, buddy. I'd like you to get married one day."

After an exaggerated swallow, Finn opened his mouth and stuck out his tongue. "Okay, can I talk now?" Sadie shook her head in disgust. "I just wanted to tell you guys that this afternoon when I got home from school I had the biggest defecation of my life."

Sadie slid another slice of pizza on her plate, picked up her plate and drink, and slowly walked away from the table. I scratched an invisible itch on my neck, and Wes ran his hand down his chin as if he had a long, thick beard.

Finn continued as if this was normal dinner conversation, "I was just thinking about how farmers use animal poop as fertilizer. We depend on it, right? So what if we could use human poop to—"

"No," I interrupted.

"But, Mom . . ."

"No," Wes and I said in unison.

Finn's eyes narrowed and his shoulders dropped. "You're stifling my creativity. What if I can cure Grandma?" What if human poop is the key to—"

"No," we said again.

There are kids who, at a very young age, start taking apart all the electronic devices in the home just to see how they work and if they can put them back together. There are kids who after helping bake their first batch of cookies are hooked and know without a doubt they want to grow up and be a baker. Then there's my kid who, after noticing changes in his grandma, decided he was meant to find a cure for Alzheimer's disease. It started with him looking under rocks in the backyard; perhaps there was an undiscovered fungus or a bug that no one had thought to extract its gunky innards and test its regenerative value.

One time Wes found Finn on the kitchen counter dumping cicada shells in our coffee grinder. He had planned on emptying LuAnne's salt shaker and refiling it with the powdered shells. As Wes turned the coffee grinder over into the trash can, Finn guilted his father by saying, "Now we'll never know if cicadas hold the key to ending good-forgetters."

Finn, once again talking with his mouth full, asked, "Can I at least have my mold back? I want to study it more."

"Oh, Finn," What was I supposed to say? I couldn't remember the lie I was going to tell him. "I'm sorry, I misplaced it."

"What? Mom, how do you misplace a baggie full of mold?"

"I'm busy, honey. I'm juggling a lot of plates right now."

Suddenly, Wes started laughing, "Wait. That was you? It was you, wasn't it?"

"What?"

"I got a call this morning from Tedd at the post office . . ."

"Wes, could we talk about this later?" I covered my face from Finn's line of sight and mouthed, "PLEASE, NO!"

"It all makes sense now," he continued to laugh, "I should have known it was you."

"Dad, what are you talking about?"

I slid my chair back, aggressive farting noises echoed through the room. There was nowhere to go. Why did I think an open floor plan was a good idea? I rushed to the refrigerator and opened the door, standing there, hidden from sight for a moment of privacy. Wes came up behind me and wrapped his arms around my waist.

"It was totally you," he whispered, still laughing. "You dropped his mold in the mail slot!"

"Stop it." I slapped at his arm.

"How did that even happen?" His face was snug in my hair; his breath and laughter warm on my neck. "I mean, really? How did that happen?"

"Shhh! It was an accident. It got mixed up with your mom's bills."

He was laughing harder now; his entire body shaking next to mine. "Tedd called because he found the baggie and thought he should report it . . . and while we were on the phone," Wes was laughing so hard he had to stop talking to catch his breath, "He said, 'Never mind, there's an apology note . . . on a napkin!'"

I turned to face him. Tears filled my eyes as I started laughing with him.

"Being normal is really hard for me," I choked as he cupped my face in his hands.

"That's what I love about you." There was silence as Wes kissed me; his lips, along with his entire body, still shaking with laughter.

"What are you guys doing?" Finn called from the table.

Wes took me by the hand and led me back to my seat.

"Finn, one day I hope you find a woman as . . . abnormal as your mom. Normal women are boring, definitely don't marry a normal woman."

"If I marry a woman that's not normal, then maybe she won't care if I talk with my mouth full!"

Laughter felt so good. We were perennials sprouting up out of the ground after a long winter's nap. I should have known, however, that the feeling wouldn't last, as with those perennials, winter's chill is always waiting around the corner sending the sprouts back into hiding. For me, it was Sadie. She stood in the entrance to her door waiting for me after I tucked Finn in for the night.

"You read my journal."

I hated it when people, especially my children, skipped the step of asking a question and went straight to an accusatory statement.

"I'm never speaking to you again," she said this with such calm. The way someone might say, "I'm going on a diet."

Without giving me a chance to confess or lie, she shot darts at me with her eyes and then closed the door in my face.

Wes was asleep when I crawled into bed. I laid there for hours listening to him breathe and staring at my parents' picture that sat on my nightstand. What would they think of this mess I've made? When my eyes finally began to blink heavy, I noticed the glowing numbers on my clock read 1:55 am. In those final moments, before the thinking turned to dreaming, the numbers on the clock blurred and blew away like dust, and for an instant, I thought I could hear my parents screaming.

Mail

I had my brother cremated. It seemed only fair. I put his ashes in the trash can. Wes pulled them out. He told me I was being . . . he couldn't think of the word, but apparently, there's a word to describe someone putting someone else's ashes in the trash. I'm certain the word was not complimentary. We contacted Nina, his ex-wife, and arranged for the ashes to be sent to her. She could put them in her trash can if she wanted. She could be the word Wes couldn't think of.

"Words are often hard to come by." That's what the preacher said at my brother's funeral. I suspect he said this because, while he had known my brother as a child, he knew nothing of him as a man. I had thought, briefly, about not having a preacher facilitate the funeral. But in the end, I did this for my parents because I knew it would make them happy, and for my brother, because I knew it would make him mad.

As the preacher stood before us, wishing words were easier to come by, I looked around the room and could only shake my head in wonder. Our parents weren't there. His fault. His ex-wife didn't come, claiming she couldn't get away. She used phrases like "big merger," "in the works," "crucial timing." His company sent representatives who claimed to be close friends. They wore tailored suits and shiny shoes that made their toes look unnaturally long. They used words like "unfathomable" and "unimaginable."

One man said he had never heard of our little town and felt a bit lost in time as he drove down the main street. Another asked how such a powerful man could come from such a place. I whispered to Wes, who wore navy blue pants and a white button down, that "classy suits don't make classy men." He kissed my forehead and said I should work that into a book sometime.

After it was all said and done, after Wes couldn't think of the word to describe me putting my brother's ashes in the trash, I thought it was over. I thought all my secrets were in the urn that would soon be Nina's responsibility. I felt relief. It is my experience, however, that relief doesn't last. Right as I was beginning to feel normal, beginning to breathe again, the other letter came.

Finn had checked the mail and said, "This one has your name on it," as he plopped the letter in Sadie's lap. I watched as she opened it, thinking, hoping it was from the summer-long honors academy she had applied to. She read the letter to herself and then stood to face me. She squinted at me, then started reading the letter again; this time in a low mumble. I asked her what it said, trying not to sound overly excited in case it was a rejection letter, which I doubted but feared all the same.

"It's from some lawyer in New York," Sadie said. "It says my biological father died, and I'm the sole heir to his inheritance." She waved the letter in the air, "What does this even mean?"

"Can we wait and have this conversation when your dad gets home?" I asked, surprised that the words came out because my tongue felt numb and my mouth had turned unusually dry.

She responded with, "Well, according to this, my dad is dead."

She glared at me, and we had an entire conversation without words. Then the life drained from her eyes, the color from her cheeks. Her lip quivered for a moment but then stopped. That's when it happened. I know because I heard it, like the crackling of ice in a cold drink; her heart hardened. It hardened so quickly I imagined a solid mass with jagged edges suspended in her chest, scraping and cutting her with every breath, every movement. If her heart stays this hard, I thought to myself, she'll kill herself from the inside out.

4

Thursday

The waiter asked, "Are you ready to order?"

"We'll need a minute," I told him. Then to my brother, "What do you want?"

"Nina wants to see her."

I shook my head, "We had an agreement."

"She doesn't want her."

"Exactly."

"That's not what I mean. Neither of us want to take her from you. But, Nina and I agree it's time for her to know the truth."

"That's not for you to decide."

"Lower your voice." He looked around the room and straightened his tie.

"This conversation is over," I said, jumping from my seat. He grabbed my arm, told me to sit down.

"I just want to talk about our options," he frowned.

"You have no options. You both signed your rights away. Sixteen years ago! This conversation is over." I stood again and made my way to the door as quickly as I could. I felt every eye in the room on me.

Outside I stood, confused, wondering if this was how LuAnne felt. Where had I parked my car? Why had I come alone? My brother was doing business in Cleveland; he didn't have time to grace our small town with his presence, so I drove the two hours to meet him, against Wes's better judgment. Now I stood, in unfamiliar territory, regretting my decision to come. I also wanted, very badly, to go back in and tell him his restaurant wasn't that great; the seats were uncomfortable and the lighting made everyone look dirty.

"Faith!" He had caught up with me, took my arm, and backed me up against the wall. My head bounced off the brick as he pushed me. He was a nose length away; his breath was hot.

"You're going to do the right thing here. She has a right to know."

I jerked my arm from his grip. I tried to walk away, but he pushed himself against me like we were in a lovers' quarrel.

"Do you know what it would do to her to find out that you're her father?" My voice shook, a sign of weakness. I hated myself for that. "I don't want her to think she's anything like you. I don't ever intend for her to know."

He pushed himself against me even harder, and I could feel that confrontation excited him, "I wanted to play nice. Let you tell her. But, maybe I should tell her myself."

"Stay away from her."

"You know, I really think she'd like to know. I think she'd like to know lots of things. You know, like how you used to invite me into your room at night."

"You were never invited." My heart was in my throat, choking me.

His mouth was too close to mine. His entire body was too close to mine. With a swift rise of my knee, he swung around and bent over in pain. I pushed myself away from the wall and frantically looked again for my car, but he was up straight again and came at me with a raised fist. I slid my hand in the side panel of my purse and pulled out my gun. My hand was shaking, as was my heart. Or maybe my heart had stopped for a moment, but something was shaking inside of me. A strange look crossed his face, perhaps it was fear. Perhaps not. In a split second, the look changed, and he smiled at me. "Oh, big girl with a gun. That's impressive. Did your policeman husband give that to you? Give it to me, and I'll show you how to use it."

I couldn't take it anymore. Or, maybe I could. But, I didn't want to. As my finger slid over the trigger, I began to step towards him. He started to step back. Wes had always told me that you never put your finger on the trigger unless you intend to pull it. I had every intention, and my brother knew it. His smile dropped. He stumbled, slightly, as he stepped off the curb. He sort of coughed, laughed, and choked all at the same time and managed to mutter one word.

Such an ugly word. Such an ugly word to be the last word you ever say. He said that one word, and then he was gone.

I woke with a start and sat up, sweat dripping down my face. I was in my bed. Wes was next to me. I was safe, though I didn't feel it. I felt sick. I went to the bathroom and sipped cold water from my hands as it poured from the faucet. I splashed my face. I hated the feeling of sticky, wet hair, so I rubbed at my face and my hair with a towel. I rubbed vigorously. My face burned. It's possible, I thought, that I rubbed off some skin. I started to cry. The tears came so quickly I felt out of control, which made me cry harder. I felt like each individual tear was a memory, a happening. Instead of wiping them away gently, I leaned forward and let them hit the floor. They splashed, breaking into a million pieces. In my own way, I was destroying the memories. I didn't want them anymore.

The longer I cried, the harder it was to breathe. My arms became numb. My legs were shaking. Pins and needles everywhere. I knew this feeling. It was anxiety. I hated anxiety. Wes had told me once that I had PTSD. I went to a counselor for a short time. He, the counselor, wore sandals with his dress pants. I thought that was dumb. He told me I had been emotionally raped. I thought that was dumb too, but later realized he was right. I now stood at the foot of my bed, staring at Wes, feeling raped.

Without turning on the light, I grabbed whatever clothes I could find and put them on. I tiptoed down the stairs and to the front door where I slipped on my tennis shoes. My purse slumped on the floor; I grabbed it and the car keys and quietly went outside. The air was crisp and refreshing, but it didn't make the rape go away. I got in my car and drove. I suppose I knew where I was going, but if anyone had asked, I'm not sure I could have said; I just went there.

By the time I reached the police station, my tears were reduced to slow, steady trickles, but my breathing remained deep and strenuous. I sat outside for a bit trying to calm myself: Inhale. 1, 2, 3, 4. Hold. 1, 2, 3, 4. Exhale. 1, 2, 3, 4. Finally, I walked to the front desk with all the confidence I could muster, well aware that I looked more like a heroin addict than the police chief's wife; I knew this because I caught my reflection in the door as I came in. No one should get dressed in the dark. No one should scrub their face with such force. No one should weep and then be seen in public with puffy eyes, a plugged nose, and chapped lips. But I did those things. All of them.

Janice sat behind the desk, typing away as if it were three in the afternoon rather than three in the morning. She looked up, let my face register and spoke with wide eyes. "Faith, are you okay? Do you need help? What's happened?"

"Oh, everything's okay. No worries. How are things here?"

She rolled her chair back from the desk and stood to face me, eye to eye.

"Everything here's fine, Faith. Is Chief Moore with you?"

"No, oh no." I quickly turned and glanced at the door, "He's home, snug in bed, fast asleep." I tapped my fingers on the high countertop. "I, um . . . well . . . I'm writing a new book."

"Oh, really," she said, her eyebrows came together.

"Yes, and I've been up all night writing, and I realized that I needed," I paused to take a deep breath, "to take a field trip."

"A field trip."

"Yeah. I'm writing about a man in prison, and I was having trouble describing his experience behind bars. I've been typing and deleting all night." Now the words were finally making some sense, or so I thought anyway. "I realized I needed to personally experience being behind bars before I could adequately describe the scene."

Janice stood motionless. I hated talking through the thick plate of glass. It seemed so impersonal. I continued, "I didn't want to wake Wes, no reason to bother him. I thought I'd just come down here and see if you'd let me spend the rest of the night . . . you know . . . behind bars."

She still didn't move.

"I know it's a strange request. I know. But you know, what is a writer if not full of . . . strange." I wrinkled my forehead, and I was certain she noticed.

"I'll tell you what." She shifted her weight and folded her arms across her chest. "I can't take you in the women's ward. But, I do have an empty bed in a holding cell. I can let you spend the rest of the night there. Will that do?"

I let out a deep sigh, not realizing I had been holding my breath. "Yes, yes that will do nicely. Thank you so much."

"You can't do any writing in there tonight; it's lights out."

"Oh, right. No writing. I'll just make notes in my head." I attempted a smile and realized my eyes were burning. Then, in my peripheral vision, I noticed strands of frizzy hair framing my face. It was too late; I decided. It was too late to be embarrassed.

Janice walked me down a short hallway and unlocked a thick metal door. As she did this it occurred to me that she could have given me the full experience, she could have searched me; which might have been unbearable and made me question why I had come here. I tasted bitter acid and grabbed my throat as if plugging a hole.

"This room is as basic as it gets." Janice turned to face me, her keys jingling. "This book you're writing . . . never mind." She squinted her eyes. "Are you sure you want to do this?"

"Positive," I whispered.

Janice closed the heavy door. I stood waiting to hear the lock turn; it took several seconds, then I heard her walk away; her shoes squeaking on the slick floor. It only took a few more seconds, and the lights dimmed. Janice should have said it was lights dimmed, not lights out. I sat on the bed, slipped off my shoes, laid down, and curled into the fetal position facing the wall. I was instantly uncomfortable and acutely aware of the hypothetical germs living in the mattress below me. To my surprise, exhaustion overcame me quickly, and I felt my body relax, it felt as though my skin and bones were melting into the bed. I almost expected to hear a sloshing sound as I spilled over the edge onto the floor. I gave myself over to the darkness and slipped into the deep.

I was aware that the air was hot and heavy. I remembered earlier that day my mom told me the AC had broken, and we'd just have to deal with the heat. I had put my hair in a bun to keep my neck cool, but I couldn't sleep without being covered, I felt too vulnerable. I had the sheet pulled up to my shoulder, and I could feel it sticking to my skin, sweat beads were trickling down my lower back and between my breasts. I heard my bedroom door open, it was louder than usual and made a sound I didn't recognize. My heartbeat became heavy, and I could feel pulsing in my temples. I was awake now but would pretend to still be sleeping. I held my breath for a moment to steady my breathing and had to be intentional about keeping my eyes closed. He was in my bedroom now, standing over me. I could hear him breathing. I hated him. I hated what was about to happen. I tensed my thighs and pressed my knees together. I felt his hand on my shoulder; heard him whisper my name.

I woke with a start, shot up, and hugged the wall, slapping his hand from my shoulder.

"Faith, baby, what are you doing?"

The light, ever so dimmed, was blinding, causing me to shield my face.

"Faith," he said again.

Wes stood over me, his arms dangling at his sides. He had on jeans and an old t-shirt. His hair was messy and dark stubble outlined his face. He looked ridiculously handsome, and amid all the thoughts running through my mind at that moment, one of them was why on earth did a guy like him choose a girl like me.

I knew I was safe, but I felt nauseous and nuzzled myself back down on the mattress and curled up in a ball. Wes wrapped himself around me as best he could on the small bed. His body was warm, his breath tickled my ear as he whispered.

"What are you doing here?"

"Janice called you, didn't she?"

"Of course Janice called me. Faith, she thought you were high or something. That's the only reason she let you in here."

I chuckled.

"It's not funny," he said, then half chuckled to himself.

"I needed to be here."

"Faith, you're scaring me."

We laid in silence for several minutes. I was fighting not to fall back asleep. I was fighting not to start crying. I was fighting not to hold my breath until I passed out. I was fighting.

"I belong here," I finally whispered.

Wes smoothed my hair with his hand like I was a cat, a gesture I found both comforting and condescending. My entire body began to shake.

"Keep talking," he whispered, tightening his grip on me.

"I've murdered him in my heart so many times. He's died a thousand deaths because of me." Wes buried his face in my hair. The words, "I'm guilty" came out in a half whisper.

"Turn around," he said to me. "I want to see you."

It took some effort in the tight space, but we managed to stretch out straight and lay face to face.

"Yes, you're guilty," he said, kissing my forehead. "But, then so am I."

He was so close his face was blurry.

"Please don't tease me," I said, wanting to wipe away my tears, but there wasn't room to move my hands to my face. I felt the salty water run down my cheeks, then my neck and well up on my collarbone.

"I'm not teasing. After all he's put you through. I've wished so many times that he would show up at my door, that I would see him behind the wheel when I pulled someone over, or that we'd meet in a dark alley. That he would antagonize me, that he would give me reason, just cause to take him down, to end him."

I didn't know what to say.

"We're all guilty, Faith."

I stared at his blurry face. For once my thoughts were utterly void.

"You didn't kill your brother," he said softly. "You're free from that. You're free to live your life outside this cell."

"There's something I haven't told you. About the night he was killed." I closed my eyes and desperately wished I was still dreaming.

"Tell me."

"We argued. He pushed me. He came at me . . ."

"I know that. You told me that."

"I pulled my gun on him."

"You did what?"

"I pulled my gun on him. I couldn't take it anymore. Or, maybe I could. But, I didn't want to."

Intertwined with a long drawn out sigh, he said my name, "Faith . . ."

In that moment I saw something in Wes I had never seen before. Fear. I knew what he was thinking, because I had thought about it myself. Besides that, it was as if his thoughts had taken shape and their silhouettes were acting out in his eyes. In the time it took him to say my name, he pictured me being interrogated, formally arrested, and the trial. What need was there for a trial when there was a confession? He thought of Sadie and Finn visiting me in prison. He thought of himself, alone at night, tormented with insomnia, consumed with worry that I was being mistreated. He searched my face and asked the question of all questions. Was his wife really a murderer?

There was nothing I could do but keep talking. Confessing. I told him the details of that fateful night. Watched the fear shift and change. Listened to his breathing quicken, then stop, then quicken again. I couldn't help but wonder if the room was wired. Was Janice listening? What did it matter, really? Wes knew the truth now, and that was all that mattered.

Wes and I stayed for some time in that holding cell, holding one another. He didn't say anything when I finally finished. He didn't say anything when he stood and took my hand, leading me off the bed and out of the cell. He didn't say anything as we passed Janice and walked out to our cars. I followed him home desperate to know what he was thinking. But, still he said nothing. Instead, he took my hand again, led me upstairs, pulled back my covers, and helped me into bed. We spent the wee hours holding one another in silence, falling in and out of sleep.

Once we heard Sadie and Finn clunking around the house, we slowly moved apart and started our day. We moved around each other with no words, just glances. Glances, I now know, can feel more intimate than just about anything. With each glance, I felt more seen, more known, and more understood than I ever had. I had shared with Wes the one thing that haunted my wake as much as my sleep. He now knew me more intimately than ever before, and more than ever before, I felt intimately known. To be known, I learned that day, is to simultaneously realize our deepest longing and greatest fear.

Confession is good for the soul, as is exhaustion. Exhaustion is one of those things that chips away at your being, forcing you to rely on someone else to get you through the day; something I had often done over the past months. That day as I dropped Finn off at school, he pushed himself between the two front seats, kissed me on the cheek, and told me I looked weary; the very word I would have used to describe Sadie that morning.

"I love you," I told her before she left the car.

She didn't respond. She just looked at me with tears in her eyes, looking weary.

As I pulled into LuAnne's driveway, the neighbor's dog ran in front of me, causing me to slam on my breaks. I heard the swooshing of movement at the same time I saw the envelope slide out from under the passenger seat. It wouldn't allow the risk of being forgotten.

"I should have put you in the trunk," I said as I pushed it back out of sight. A numbing sensation shot through my arms and legs when I touched the envelope.

I took a moment, before getting out, to breathe. Inhale. 1, 2, 3, 4. Hold. 1, 2, 3, 4. Exhale. 1, 2, 3, 4.

LuAnne, thankfully, was having a good day. She was present. I desperately needed her mind to be her own; mine was too weak to work for us both. I had whispered this on the way to her house and finding her thus so felt like an underserved and most appreciated gift. One that made me feel intimately seen, known, and understood.

She greeted me at the front door, coffee cup in hand.

"Oh my," she said the moment we locked eyes. "You need coffee worse than I do. Come in, come in."

LuAnne ushered me in and pulled out a chair. She poured a cup of coffee and set it in front of me, along with her ceramic cream and sugar set, essentials that would be among the last to be packed.

"Rough night?" she asked.

"You can say that again."

"If Finn were here, he'd say it again." We both smiled. "Do you want to talk about it?"

I just shook my head. I feared if I opened my mouth, even to say "No, thank you," I would just keep talking, keep confessing, and I had had enough of that for one day. After a moment LuAnne, in her casual way, averted my attention.

"Do you think the children will miss me in this house?"

"Eventually," I said. "Not at first. Maybe at Christmas. Christmas will be different."

She took a long sip of her coffee. "Who knew that last Christmas would be my last Christmas?" Then she added, "I mean, here, in this house. And baking cookies, I won't do that there."

"You can bake cookies at our house."

She grinned and said, "Of course. Now, tell me while I'm not so foggy, are you going to write this book?"

"What do you think I should do?"

"Well," she fingered her pearls like they were a rosary. "Forgive him." She took another sip and choked on her coffee. "Excuse me," she said, wiping at her mouth.

I looked down at my coffee and rotated the cup, making dark swirls. I then added milk, and as the colors mixed, it was like looking at my heart in liquid form. My greatest joys and my deepest wounds were mingling, mixed in the same cup. In some strange way, a way that both did and didn't make sense, they complemented one another.

"I've said for years that I've forgiven him." My words came out as a whisper.

She reached over the table and, without touching me, simply placed her hand next to mine, bringing to my attention that her forefinger, just above the top knuckle, was being tugged to the right by arthritis.

"Maybe you have. Maybe you haven't." LuAnne let out a deep, long breath, and then said, "You are like the . . . the sand. At the beach. You know there's so much litter on the beaches because people leave their trash lying around. All that trash . . . the trash is all the hurt. But, what happens?"

"What?" I asked.

"The water comes in. The . . . the tide. The tide comes in. If the tide is weak, it just moves the trash around. But, if the tide is strong, it washes the trash away. Does that make sense?"

"The tide is forgiveness," I said.

"Yes, precisely. The sand looks different now. It's never the same after the tide comes. But, it's cleaner. Do you see?" She stood and refilled her coffee cup. "It does no good to withhold forgiveness from someone who isn't here anymore. Not forgiving them doesn't teach them a lesson once they're dead, you know what I mean? You aren't hurting the person back; you're only hurting yourself, causing yourself more pain. Do you see?"

I looked at LuAnne, into her gentle eyes, and for a brief moment she was herself again; whole and full of wisdom. She stared back at me and, unlike so many days, I could tell she saw me, really saw me, the way she did before, back when life made sense.

"Do you see?" she asked again.

"Yes, I see." I looked out the window; it was starting to sprinkle.

"I love the rain," LuAnne whispered. "One time Vernon and I were outside and it started raining. I wanted to run inside because of my hair, you know. Vernon asked me to stay. He wrapped his arms around me and kissed me." She ran her fingers over her lips. "He held me there with the rain coming down so hard it hurt. He told me he had always wanted to make love to me in the rain. I wanted to too. But the neighbors, you see, the neighbors were so close, I just couldn't do it." She spun her wedding ring around her thin finger, then said, "That's probably the only thing I regret. In all my life that's the one thing, I regret not making love to Vernon in the rain that day."

Picturing Vernon and LuAnne young and in love wasn't difficult. The difficult part was imagining only having one regret. One. And for that one regret to be not making love to your husband in the rain a million years ago. I couldn't even begin to list off my regrets, and I certainly couldn't reduce them down to one; it simply couldn't be done. I envied LuAnne for this. Whether she truly had no other regrets or if she did and just couldn't remember them, I envied her. LuAnne and I would spend the morning looking at her life, all taped up in boxes, and finish packing her personal bag that would accompany her to River Side. She would be joining us for dinner that night and had agreed to help me make her famous lasagna; her cooking skills being something else I envied.

At the grocery store, LuAnne said she would get the French bread and meet me at the spaghetti sauce. She was thinking clearly enough that I didn't argue. As I watched LuAnne walk away, on her mission to find French bread, I realized I was standing next to a coffee display. The aroma was intoxicating, and I couldn't help but run my fingers across the open barrel of coffee beans, letting the smooth pods kiss my skin. Then I saw them, little cellophane bags tied with black ribbon. I grabbed one, untied the bow, and inhaled as deeply as possible, with my nose in the bag. I decided as I stood there savoring the scent, that whoever thought to coat espresso beans in chocolate should be celebrated. Not just mentioned in passing but celebrated with a statue or perhaps a national holiday. I tied the ribbon and tossed it along with two more bags into my cart before moving on.

In aisle four, with me praying LuAnne could find the bread, I placed a jar of spaghetti sauce in my cart and looked up to see a woman walking toward me. It was Claire's mom, Jillian. She wore a knee-length pencil skirt, a silk blouse, and high heels, her nails perfectly manicured. She worked as an assistant to her husband at his chiropractic office, something that always amused me. I felt that he, her chiropractic husband, should tell her those heels didn't do her back any favors. She wasn't from here, Jillian; she was from the city and had apparently worked as a fashion model. When word spread that Jackson Tiddle was moving back with his wife to open his own practice, all the ladies were curious and giddy, as if waiting to meet her was something like waiting to open a birthday gift. But, when word spread that his wife was a model from the city, all the ladies secretly decided to hate her and forbid their husbands to enter Jackson Tiddle's business. This was ridiculous as Jackson Tiddle was the only chiropractor in our town, and you can only envy the assistant for so long when you desperately need an adjustment. The first time I met her, going on thirteen years ago now, she was in a tight black dress that made me look at the floor; we were at the library for story hour. I remember at one point during the story stealing a quick glance at her dress, her high heels, and long sleek legs, and I understood why all the women decided to hate her. But then she smiled, and I saw she had lipstick on her teeth. Because she made me feel less than I was, I knew we would never be friends, but because of the lipstick on her teeth, I decided not to hate her. It's always been ironic to me that our daughters became inseparable.

That day, in the grocery store, I looked at her with her perfect everything and wondered if there was something else there, something I would want to be inseparable from if I dug deep enough. Maybe whatever Sadie saw in Claire I could see in her mom if I tried, should I ever find myself wanting to spend quality time with someone who made me feel shorter than I actually was.

She caught me staring and said, "Oh, hello, Faith." I tugged at my wrinkled t-shirt and was suddenly aware that I wasn't wearing makeup.

"Thank you," I said, slowly pushing my cart towards her, "thank you for having Sadie over for the weekend."

"Oh, no need to thank me," she smiled with her perfect teeth and perfectly shaded lipstick. "We all just love Sadie. She's such a sweet young lady. I am sorry though that she's having such a hard time right now. Sadie, Claire, and I . . . well, we sat on the back deck with some ice cream and had a good long talk about it." She stood tall and straight with her well-adjusted spine.

I assumed Sadie would confide in her best friend that her parents had been lying to her for sixteen years about who she really was, that her uncle was her real dad. I figured she'd cry on Claire's shoulder and call Wes and me names she would later regret, but it never occurred to me that she would tell Claire's mother too. What on earth did Jillian think of me? I leaned on the cart for balance.

"Kyle was such a sweet boy," she said, leaning toward me.

"Excuse me? What about Kyle?" I cocked my head to the side.

"Kyle. Sadie and Kyle broke up." She put her hand to her mouth but was careful not to touch her lips. "I assumed you knew. She didn't tell you?"

My hand went to my throat, and I let out a quick bark of laughter. Claire's mom leaned back, and her eyes went wide for a second. "Well, I've been spending a lot of time with my mother-in-law." My voice was shaking, so I stopped talking. I looked down at my feet and realized I could hear myself breathing. "She's moving into River Side, tomorrow actually. My mother-in-law, not Sadie." I rolled my eyes at myself. "So, Sadie and I haven't had our usual time together; you know, to talk."

Claire's mom nodded and grinned with her lips pressed together. Then with narrowed eyes said, "She's really struggling emotionally. I think you should make time for her soon." Without thinking, I squeezed the handle of my cart and shoved it forward causing Claire's mom to take several steps back. Suddenly a sharp pain shot through my clenched jaw. I felt a scream welling up inside of me, one that had needed to come out for some time. Perhaps it was the same storm that had been brewing since I was ten years old. I bit both of my lips to hold in the scream, so it came out my hands instead. I started to give the cart another good heave, and then I froze. Every inch of me, including the cart, froze. It was as if the voice inside had become more than a voice and was physically restraining me. Claire's mom stood with her mouth open, something I doubt she did often. She touched her forehead then pushed her hair back off her shoulder. "Are you okay? Do you need help?"

"Clearly" is what I wanted to say but couldn't.

LuAnne came down the aisle behind Claire's mom and put the bread in my cart. I could feel the grip loosening as LuAnne looked up and said, "Hello there, I'm LuAnne."

Claire's mom blinked a heavy blink and said, "I'm Jillian."

"Nice to meet you, Jillian. You must be friends with Faith." She glanced at me and then exclaimed, "My goodness, Faith. Are you okay?"

I cleared my throat and stood as tall as I could. The words, "I'm fine" came out in a half whisper. I closed my eyes, praying that this was all a dream, but when I opened my eyes, LuAnne and the perfect woman named Jillian were still standing there, staring at me. I cleared my throat again and spoke more normally this time. "Really, I'm okay. I just had a . . . It's been a long week. I'm a little tired."

"You're more than tired. You're exhausted!" LuAnne touched Jillian's arm as if they were old friends, "Faith's been helping me move, the poor thing isn't getting enough rest. And then on top of helping me, she's dealing with Sadie and her broken heart. What was the boy's name? Kevin? Kyle? Kyle, wasn't it? The poor girl."

Jillian raised her eyebrows and smirked.

"You know about Kyle?" Everything went blurry.

"Of course I do. Sadie called me the night they broke up. She was distraught."

Before Wes and I had children, I would shudder at the thought of me dying young and Wes remarrying. I wanted him to be happy, sure, but the thought of him sharing the deep things of the heart with another woman made me feel sick inside. After we became parents, I realized it wasn't just about Wes having a new wife, I also didn't want another woman caring for my children, them giving away pieces of their hearts that were meant for me. These are, obviously, selfish thoughts; but even so, these are thoughts I've had.

And now here I was, standing in the grocery store, looking at two women who knew something about my daughter that I didn't know. And not just any old thing, but a deep thing of the heart. It occurred to me, in that incredibly awkward moment, that perhaps I had it all wrong, as we most often do when consumed with our own selfish thoughts. I was reminded, by the voice inside, that I had confided—many times—in LuAnne rather than my own mother, that she, LuAnne, knew the deep things of my heart; things my own mother didn't know. The word hypocrite came to mind; the same word my brother had used countless times to describe the people in our town; the reason, he always said, he couldn't wait to get away. He was right; I was a hypocrite. Not only that but maybe, just maybe, Wes would be better off, happier even, with a new wife and maybe, most likely, our children would benefit from a new mother. With this in mind, I said to the voice inside, "I'm okay to go. This might be the best time. It might be best for me to die, right here in aisle four with the spaghetti sauce."

I didn't die. My heart kept beating even though it was broken, a phenomenon I will never understand—another side effect of guilt, I suppose, being kept alive when you don't deserve to be. I stood there, undeservingly alive, wondering how to get away, and I suddenly understood why children like curling up on the rack underneath the shopping cart. I would rather, in that moment, have been staring at LuAnne and Jillian's feet rather than their faces. I pictured Sadie as a toddler simply closing her eyes to play hide and seek, thinking that if she couldn't see me, I couldn't see her. I desperately wished it worked that way; I would be closing my eyes often.

"We should go," I said to LuAnne, as kindly as I could.

She quickly looked at Jillian and with a smile and a pat on the arm said, "It was so nice running into you today. Have a good afternoon." Jillian stood frozen as if her heels had been superglued to the floor and watched us walk away.

We made our way to the checkout lane, LuAnne acting as if nothing had happened, me wondering if the store had security cameras and imagining the employees having a good laugh at my expense and asking, "Isn't she a Moore?" All I wanted was to get out of that store as quickly as possible and with no additional stress. But, that just isn't how my life works. As I bent over the cart and grabbed the spaghetti sauce, I looked up and found my brother staring me straight in the eye. I dropped the jar of sauce back in the cart and gasped as prickles ran the full length of my body. The headline read, "His incredible life, his tragic death. What really happened that fateful night?" I reached for the magazine, then pulled my arm back. Behind me, LuAnne was flipping through the sudoku books, in front of me a woman was swiping her credit card, and I didn't see any cameras overhead, so I reached for the magazine a second time but again recoiled. Biting both my lips and with shaking hands, I quickly grabbed the magazine and turned it backward. I stood with my hands on my chest staring at the Ford ad on the back cover until the trance was interrupted by my cell phone ringing. As I dug in my purse, LuAnne stepped in and began placing my groceries, one item at a time and with the speed of a snail, on the conveyor belt. It was the elementary school calling. They needed me to come immediately.

At the elementary school, LuAnne said, "Someone should stay with the groceries, don't you think?" I left the car windows cracked, as if she were a pet, and hurried into the main entrance. Finn sat outside the principal's office reading a book, his legs swaying with ease under the chair. I had just reached his side when the door opened, and principal King said in her monotone voice, "Mrs. Moore, Finn, would you please join me in my office." At Mrs. King's prompting, we all sat down, and my eyes went to the bowl of chocolates on her desk. My mouth began to water, and I wondered, for a moment, if I was allowed to take one.

"Mrs. Moore, I've called you in today because Finn was caught fighting with a classmate in the hallway, and I think you know we don't tolerate that sort of behavior here at Mooreville Elementary."

"You were fighting?" I quickly looked him over head to toe while asking, "Are you hurt?"

"I'm not hurt, and it was necessary," he said, flipping through the pages of his book. I half expected the next words out of his mouth to be, "And yes, I know, our ancestors are shaking their heads in shame."

"Please explain yourself," Mrs. King said, folding her arms over her chest. "And would you mind putting your book down?"

Finn plopped his book in his lap, scratched his forehead, and said matter of factly, "Keaton called Sadie a slut. I was defending her honor."

Mrs. King unfolded her arms and sat up straighter in her chair.

"Finn," I said, leaning towards him, "Do you even know what the word slut means?"

"He was implying that Sadie is promiscuous."

"How do you know what promiscu . . . never mind."

"Mom, he called Sadie a slut, so I pushed him. I didn't anticipate him hitting me back, which I realize now was the most logical outcome. But when he hit me, I had to defend myself; the punches just kept coming."

I covered my face with my hands; an upflow of acid burned my throat, causing me to cough.

"Finn." Principal King walked around her desk and knelt by Finn's chair. "I understand why you did what you did. On the one hand, your actions are admirable. Your sister is lucky to have a brother who will stand up for her. But, on the other hand, violence is never the answer, and that's just not how we deal with conflict here at Mooreville Elementary. I'm sending you home for the remainder of the day so that you can think about what you've done. I would also like a 500-word essay on how your forefathers, the men who founded Mooreville, would feel about your actions today."

Finn glared at me and wrinkled his forehead in disbelief, then said to Mrs. King, "I'd love to write an essay about my forefathers, about how they'd be proud that I defended the Moore name. I'll have it for you first thing in the morning."

"Finn," I put my hand on his knee and squeezed it, "be respectful."

"Be respectful?" he snapped, "Keaton is the one being disrespectful, not me!"

"Finn . . ."

"You're right," Mrs. King interrupted. "Keaton was disrespectful."

"So then, does Keaton have to go home early and write an essay?" he asked, cocking his head to the side. When Mrs. King didn't answer, he threw up his hands and muttered, "This is inequitable."

"You struck first," Mrs. King said firmly.

Finn slouched down in defeat and leaned his head back on the chair. His Adam's apple was becoming more pronounced; he was growing up too quickly for my liking.

"Finn, why don't you wait for your mom in the hallway. I'd like to speak to her alone for a moment."

He slid from the chair, his book in one hand, his backpack in the other and without a word, left the room.

"Mrs. Moore, I hope you understand—"

I interrupted her because I understood all too well, "Mrs. King, my mother-in-law is waiting for us in the car, so I have to go."

At the door, she called, "Faith," as if we were friends. I turned to her, and she asked, "Is everything okay at home?"

Once again those relentless tears presented themselves; I quickly turned my back to her. "Faith, if there's something going on at home . . ."

She didn't finish her sentence; I wanted to ask, "What? If there's something going on at home, what? What can you do about it?"

"Everything's fine," I lied and left her office, my heart beating so fast I could hear the rush of blood and felt deep pressure in the back of my head. I steadied myself with my hand on the wall until I saw the secretary staring at me. I forced a smile, pushed off the wall, and met Finn in the hallway. Taking his backpack, I asked with a shaky voice, "Who is Keaton anyway? Does he even know Sadie?"

"He's Kyle's little brother. Keaton said that Kyle and Sadie broke up because Sadie's a slut."

My hand went to my stomach; the burning had gotten so bad I imagined a hole forming and my insides spilling out, something I would hate for Finn to see.

"Mom, I don't think we should tell Sadie about this. I mean, now I know why she cries at night. But, it'll just make her more miserable to know Kyle's talking bad about her."

"I think you're right," I told him, squeezing his shoulder. "You have a good heart." He gave me a toothy grin and started bobbing his head as he walked.

"What's this?" LuAnne asked as Finn climbed in the back seat. "Is there trouble?"

Finn let out a breath and said, "Apparently they punish boys for being chivalrous and defending their sister's honor."

"Oh, my." LuAnne looked at me; I held up my hand and simply shook my head. "In my day," she continued, "it was expected that a young man would stand up for his sister's honor."

"Those were the days, Grandma. Those were the days."

Finn was right; those were the days; the days when all mothers wore heels to the grocery store, and none of them lost their temper and acted like psychopaths. Abusive men weren't celebrated on the cover of magazines, and you could expect to be punched if you dare talk bad about someone else's sister. Those were the days, and those days were long gone.

As I stood beside LuAnne that evening assembling her famous lasagna, I was reminded of other days long gone. The night before my parents traveled to New York, Wes and my dad stood over the grill flipping burgers. In the kitchen my mom sat at the counter snapping beans; she fussed over me when I burned my fingers pulling baked potatoes from the oven. Had I known that would be our last meal together, I would have planned something more. I would have listened closer, hugged tighter, and said more than, "See you when you get back." I looked at LuAnne now and was painfully aware that one day, one of these meals, would be our last. Our last smile, our last conversation, our last hug would inevitably come.

"Are you okay?" LuAnne placed her hand on my back.

I faked a smile and said, "I'm fine."

"What about you, Finn?" she smiled at him, and I noticed her head shook a bit, involuntarily. "What are you reading over there? You look engrossed."

His eyes stayed on the page as he lowered the book to his lap. "Well, basically there are these two boys who are lost in the bush in Africa. They've been trying to find their way back to town to where they hope their parents are, but they're being stalked by a lion, and so they can't cover much ground. They're spending most of their time hiding."

"This isn't true, is it?" She lifted a hand towards her pearls but then lowered it again, examining the spaghetti sauce on her fingers.

"No, Grandma. It's fiction."

She let out a deep nervous breath, "Go on then."

"The boys figured out that the land wouldn't let them leave, not without something in return. The land needed a sacrifice. So, they made up a ceremonial dance, but it didn't work. Then they made up a song, then a chant, then they braided different leaves and grasses together and laid it on a big rock like it was an altar. But, nothing worked."

"Oh, my," LuAnne looked from me to Finn with big eyes. "This sounds serious. What do you suppose they'll do?"

"I don't know, Grandma. There's only one more chapter, so I'll find out soon. Next time I see you, I'll tell you how it ended."

She said nothing, but after wiping her hands began fingering her pearls.

Wes walked in the door just as the house began to smell like an Italian restaurant. "Am I in the right house?" he asked. "Oh, my mother must be here. The house only smells this good when my mother is here." Wes winked at me and shook his head as he hugged her. When he let go and tried to take a step back, she took his face in her hands and held it there, studying him. At last, she patted his cheek and told him to go change; he wouldn't want to risk sloping red sauce on his uniform. He returned with Sadie trailing behind him; her shoulders slumped, her face flushed.

"Sadie . . ." Before I could say anything more, she walked into her grandmother's arms, resting her head on LuAnne's shoulder.

"Oh, my." LuAnne pushed Sadie back and placed a hand on her forehead. "You have a fever. Are you not feeling well?"

"We thought it was just her period," I answered for her, "but now I'm not so sure."

Wes and I took turns feeling Sadie's forehead, surprised that she allowed either of us to touch her.

"I'll be fine," she said in a half whisper. Then to her grandmother, "Really. I'll be fine."

At the dinner table, I couldn't help but notice that Sadie would take a bite, and then cover her mouth to chew and swallow. She only took a handful of bites before asking to be excused. I couldn't help but think we should have LuAnne over more often if it meant Sadie's manners returning.

"You go and lie down," LuAnne said to her, "I'll come check on you before I go home."

Sadie attempted a smile and made her way up the stairs, one step at a time, holding onto the railing. Wes and I exchanged a glance, and in that moment when our eyes locked I thought to myself that I would take Sadie to Urgent Care in the morning, Wes nodded in agreement.

"I hope whatever Sadie has isn't highly contagious." Finn ran a napkin across his mouth, "I'm really not in the mood to be sick right now."

"Speaking of you," LuAnne said with a smile, "I have something for you. I almost forgot." Reaching into her pocket, she pulled out a small, green pocket knife and handed it to Finn from across the table.

"No way! For me?"

"Oh, LuAnne . . ." I attempted to interject.

Wes cleared his throat to get my attention and mouthed, "It's okay."

"I needed a pocket knife, how did you know?"

"A little bird told me," she said, winking at Wes. I put my hands on my chest, hoping the pressure would calm my heart. Before I could take another breath Finn was around the table giving his grandmother a hug, her making him promise to be careful and not run with the blade out. I just shook my head, and Wes mouthed again that it was okay.

How did he know it was okay? I wanted to ask him this. I wanted to tell Finn to give it back; he couldn't keep it. But then LuAnne explained that it had belonged to Vernon and that Finn should take extra good care of it so that one day he could give it to his own son. She pulled the dead-grandfather-heirloom card, and then I couldn't tell him to give it back. I pressed harder against my chest and closed my eyes to avoid Wes mouthing again that it was okay. The problem, I realized, was that I was too hungry to just sit there with my eyes closed, and no one wanted to see me haphazardly try and blindly feed myself. My eyes, just like my hands, have clearly been underappreciated.

I opened my eyes to find Wes and LuAnne eating their lasagna without a care in the world, while Finn slathered extra butter on his garlic bread with his grandfather's knife that had been who knows where. I rubbed my hands down my jeans and then pushed my hair away from my face. As I sat there, I was reminded of how badly a bright light hurts your eyes first thing in the morning, but over time—and usually not very much time—your eyes adjust, and you see clearly; the instinct to squint is no longer needed, forgotten. I was reminded of this because the longer I sat there, the more comfortable I became. My heart beat a little slower, and my glances toward Finn became less frequent. It was okay.

After dinner LuAnne made her way upstairs to check on Sadie, Finn sat on the floor trying to slice pieces of paper with his new knife, and Wes stood behind me at the sink with his arms around my waist.

"I'm exhausted," he whispered, burying his face in the crook of my neck. I let out a deep breath and started to say, "Me too," but I didn't. My exhaustion didn't trump his exhaustion, and he needed, at that moment, to bury his face in my neck and lean into me as if I were holding him up.

"Thank you for doing so much for my mom," he said, his words tickling my skin. "Do you still think moving her is the right thing?"

Do I still think moving her is the right thing? "It's a little late to be asking that," I wanted to say. But instead, I leaned my head against his and whispered, "Yes."

I heard LuAnne walk back in the kitchen and immediately noticed her watery eyes as I turned to face her.

"Wesley, dear, I'm ready to go home now, if you please." Then she took me in her arms and kissed me on the cheek. "Oh, I almost forgot. I have something for you too." She opened her purse and began digging around inside; what she pulled out was wrapped in a paper towel. "This is for you," she said, placing it in my hand.

Inside the paper towel was her mother's broach.

"LuAnne . . ." She shushed me before I could utter another word.

"I want you to have it." She smiled sweetly then looked at Finn, who was now slicing the air instead of paper. "I have a gift for everyone." She then looked up at the ceiling as we stood below Sadie's bedroom, and it was then I noticed she was no longer wearing her pearl necklace. "I've heard stories about River Side," she said, clasping her purse, "Maybe people lose things or maybe the employees have sticky fingers. Either way, I don't want to take anything of real value with me. I want my family to have them. I want you to have my mother's broach, and I want you to think of me every time you wear it." She patted my cheek, holding my gaze just long enough for my tears to rise up, and then she turned, took Wes's arm, and let him escort her home.

By 9:00, Finn was in bed, angry that I wouldn't let him sleep with his new pocket knife. Sadie still hadn't come out of her room; she was still angry with me too. I had reclined on the couch with the chocolate covered espresso beans and was through one bag when Wes walked in, his dad's Citizen of the Year certificate tucked under his arm. He smiled at me and winked; it was then I realized my heart was beating fast and extra heavy. Was the sudden excitement inside from Wes or the caffeine in the espresso beans? A woman can never be sure of such things.

"It's starting to rain again," Wes said, leaning the large picture frame against the wall. He plopped down next to me and, with a great deal of effort, managed to get his large fingers in the tiny bag I held and pull out an espresso bean.

"Oh, these are good." He grabbed another one. "Where have these been all my life?"

I handed him the bag, stood, and crossed the room.

"This can't go on forever, you know. Sadie being so angry. Maybe we should see a family therapist or something."

Wes tugged at his invisible beard again. "I say we give it a little more time. But, I trust your . . ." he waved his hand at me, "your woman's intuition or whatever. So, if you think we need to see a therapist, we'll see a therapist."

"Maybe we should install a camera in her room. I can't stand not knowing what she's doing up there."

"Okay, no. No cameras in her room."

"Oh, come on. You have to have little spy cameras at the office. What if she's hurting herself? What if she's doing drugs or something?"

"You wanna know what she's doing up there? She's writing in her journal or she's drawing pictures. Or, maybe she's on the phone telling Kyle how much she hates us. Who knows. But, I don't think she's hurting herself, and I'm confident she's not doing drugs."

"Did you know she and Kyle broke up?"

"What? No. When did that happen?"

I didn't answer, instead I opened the front door and stepped outside. "I'll be back."

"You'll be back? Where are you going?" As I stepped onto the lawn I heard him ask, "Are you going to the post office? Do you have more mold that needs mailing?"

I walked around the house, and as I looked up at Sadie's window, the rain began to fall harder. Her light was on but the curtains were drawn.

Wes stepped around the corner and called my name. Without taking my eyes off Sadie's window, I extended my arm, reaching for Wes. He came to me without hesitation and stood with me in the rain. He would always have my love. Then, now, and forever, because of this.

After several minutes, soaked to the bone, I turned from the window and wrapped my arms around Wes. "Do you want to make love to me?"

"Yes."

"Now?"

"Yes."

"Here?"

"What?"

"Do you want to make love to me? Now, here . . . right here in the backyard, in the rain?"

"Y . . . es. But, no." He looked around, "What about the neighbors?"

"So, you'd be happier in the house? In our bedroom?" I asked excitedly.

"Much. Much happier. Why are you smiling?"

"Because I can check this off my list."

"Your list?"

"I have a long . . . a very long list of regrets. But, I'm happy that neglecting to make love to you in the rain won't be on that list."

He stared at me for what seemed like an eternity. Then, because he knows me so well, he started wiping the wet hair away from my face.

"Being normal really is hard for you, isn't it?"

I shook my head yes, took him by the hand, and led him up to our bed. It was him, I decided, that had my heart pumping.

The Note

"I don't know," my mom said innocently, "I just told him I was throwing you a baby shower and that maybe he'd want to at least send you a card or something."

"Mom, why would you do that?"

"Well, I don't know. I thought maybe it would give him some closure or something."

All I could do was shake my head. She went to her purse and pulled out an envelope. She had a look of satisfaction on her face and said, "Well, it must have been an okay idea because he did it. See, he sent you a card."

She handed me the envelope and then put her hand on my arm. Her lower lip disappeared into her upper lip, and as her eyes squinted, they began to water. She tilted her head slightly as if to say, "This is an important thing you're holding in your hand. Your brother labored over this, choosing each word thoughtfully and with care. Here, in this envelope, are the words of a hurting man; words that describe his heartache and perhaps even a twinge of regret but yet also the comfort and joy he has knowing his daughter will be well loved and cared for. Perhaps Nina wrote something too, you never know. You just never know what kind of emotion might be poured out into this card. You will keep this forever; this will be the card you give to Sadie one day to help her understand why her parents made the decision they did. This card is everything."

All of this she said to me; all of this she said without words but with the secret language mothers and daughters share. I felt these unspoken words travel through her hand and into my arm, which then traveled through my entire body with a warmth, like meds through an IV. But, soon the warmth dissipated, and I began to feel sick. I lowered my arm so that she would let go, and then I told her I would save the card and open it later in private. Such a thing should be read when I had time to give it my full attention. She nodded, wiped her eyes, and walked away.

Later that evening, while preparing dinner, I opened the envelope and found a single white piece of paper folded in half. On the paper, in my brother's still boyish handwriting, was simply written, "You're welcome."

I tore the paper in half and tossed it in the trash. After dinner, I slopped the remains of spaghetti and meatballs on top of the torn paper. I never told my mom what the note said. Two years later my parents would die thinking my brother and I had shared a special connection through that card, that one day Sadie would understand everything, that her eyes would be opened after reading the words he had labored over to express himself so perfectly. My parents would die not knowing the truth, which wasn't the worst thing.

The worst thing, other than not watching Sadie grow up, was that my parents never met Finn; something that grieved me so deeply I rarely allowed myself to think the thoughts. They would have loved Finn, and Finn would have loved them; tremendously. Over the years I've created, on rare occasions, images in my mind of my dad taking Finn fishing or my mom buying him ice cream; black cherry to be exact, as that was her favorite. These were fake images that I've revisited just enough times that they almost seem real, like photos that I've seen but misplaced so that I can't prove the memories really happened, but I feel very strongly in my heart that they did.

There are actual pictures, in albums on my living room shelves, of my parents and Sadie. Two wonderful years of memories, the documentation of their love for her. I know, though I was never told, that my mom sent pictures of Sadie to my brother. I knew this because I knew my mom. I knew when she laughed while taking a picture, she was freezing memories for herself. I knew when she took a picture with tears in her eyes that she was freezing memories for him; memories he didn't ask for, and I've wondered if he even looked at them or kept them; if he cherished them. I've wondered if over the years, he longed for more or if he even noticed they stopped coming. I've wondered how he knew—seven years later without my mom there to tell him—that we had finally gotten pregnant.

Soon after Finn was born I remember flipping through the mail and coming across a white envelope. My name had been typed on a mailing label and was stuck on at a slight angle. There was no return address, but the stamp had been postmarked in New York City. Seeing that made my heart flutter, but not in a good way like the way a woman's heart flutters when she receives a letter of affection or something that is sure to be good news, but rather the way a heart flutters when standing too close to the edge of a cliff. I opened the letter immediately, still standing in the yard, wanting to get it over with. There was though, just as there had been with my mom, a bit of naivety that made me wonder if this was the apology I had long been waiting for. Could this be the letter he poured over, choosing his words thoughtfully and with care? Had he realized, finally, his part in our parent's death? Had he finally wanted to speak about the unspeakable?

Inside the envelope was another plain white sheet of paper folded in half. In that same rushed handwriting were the words, "Congratulations. You finally figured out how to make a baby without me."

I tore the letter into as many pieces as I possibly could, then I threw them on the ground and stomped on them; jumping up and down and grunting like a toddler throwing a temper tantrum. After several minutes I looked down and was surprised to see the pieces still on the ground—surely the force of my stomping had disintegrated them! I picked the pieces up in one quick swoop and ran to the end of the driveway and down the street in front of the neighbor's house. I bent over and shoved them down the storm drain, saying things to the pieces, things I wouldn't normally say, as they disappeared into the black hole. As I stood straight again, I gave the drain one last stomp and then caught movement from the corner of my eye. It was old Mrs. Higbea watching me from her front window.

What I knew about Mrs. Higbea, from gossip not because she told me herself, was that her only son fought in Vietnam and returned home severely disabled. "Where was he wounded?" people would ask. "He doesn't look wounded," others would say. Lawrence, her son, would be seen around town with full use of his arms and legs, with his spotless skin and full head of wavy hair, looking as healthy as anyone else. "He was wounded in his soul," his mother would tell people. "He was wounded in his soul."

On occasion, so I've heard, Lawrence would wake the neighbors with his night terrors. He might be found wandering in their backyard howling at the moon like a dog or lying in the grass screaming, tightly holding himself in the fetal position. He would, from time to time, accompany his mother to the grocery store and for no apparent reason start stomping on the ground and cursing. Although Mrs. Higbea and her son have been dead for some time now, I still think back on that day, me stomping in my front yard and then having a fit over the storm drain. I can still see the look on her face; a look of remembrance, familiarity, understanding, and something else—fear, perhaps. I felt shame for not having control over my emotions and for causing her what I believed to be pain. I felt shame then, and I feel shame now—for this.

Wes held me that night while I cried. He understood I was upset over the card from my brother but that my tears were brought on by my own actions. "I had no right," I told him, "I had no right to act that way, given what Lawrence had gone through. Lawrence had every right."

Wes held me, and when there were no more tears, he told me this: "Trauma can't be compared." Lawrence had fought a war that he had no desire to fight. He had been drafted; he had not wanted to be there. He spent time as a prisoner of war and not only saw but heard things that we simply cannot comprehend. His trauma was real, and it was his burden to bear. Then he told me that I too had fought my own war and had been a prisoner in my own home. I didn't want to experience the things that were forced on me, but I did, and I survived, just as Lawrence had. My trauma was real, and it was my burden to bear. Our trauma is our own, and our response is our own. There was no room for comparison. There simply was no room.

The following day I baked a loaf of banana bread and offered it to Mrs. Higbea; my way of apologizing and wanting her to see me in good spirits. She offered me tea, and we sat on her front porch enjoying a snack in the cool breeze. We spoke of her late husband, of my parents and how Sadie was adjusting to having a baby in the house. We spoke of God and of her next hair appointment, where she would get, as always, a tight perm. We spoke of everything and of nothing, and when I told her I needed to get home, Mrs. Higbea took me in her arms and whispered in my ear that she was sorry, so very sorry, that I had been wounded in my soul.

5

Friday

I stood in front of the foggy mirror in our bathroom. My hair was wet and stuck to my face, a feeling I hated. I pushed my hair back and realized how the older I got, I looked more and more like my mother. I have wished over the years that memories only came to mind when called upon. But we all know that's not how it works. A smell, a touch, a stranger's laugh can flood us with unexpected memories. On this morning, as I stood in astonishment at my resemblance to my mother, I remembered her. Her and my father, in their living room, sitting across from Wes and I. My mom was crying. My dad sat staring out the window; the weight of the world on his shoulders.

"We'll take her," I said. "No question." I looked to Wes; he repeated my words, "No question."

"Mom?"

I stepped out of the bathroom and found Finn coming at me. "I'm up," I said to him, pleased that he wasn't waking me up to remind me of that place he has to go every day at the same time.

"Would you please make eggs for breakfast?" he asked, stopping only long enough to make puppy dog eyes at me. Walking away, he said over his shoulder, "I'm a growing boy, and I need protein."

In the kitchen I found Sadie sitting at the bar watching a movie on her laptop.

"I'm making eggs, want some?"

She didn't answer. I'd make enough for her even if she didn't eat them.

"What's that you're watching?" I asked, hoping to sound interested and not like a snooping mother.

She sighed. "It's an old movie Claire told me to watch."

As I placed the skillet on the range, I heard a woman's voice say, "You greedy Americans. You think you are so entitled." I then recognized Diane Lane's voice as she responded with a sweet, "Some of us feel really badly about that."

"Under the Tuscan Sun," I said. I also wanted to say, "It's not that old." But, maybe it was.

"You've seen this?" Sadie asked.

"I have. It was one of my favorites."

"Huh."

I sprayed the skillet with canola oil and one by one the eggs began to sizzle as they hit the hot surface. I cracked the last egg, and as a bloody yolk fell in its place, I said, "Ugh" just as Diane Lane said, "Ugh" to the bird that had just pooped on her head.

The old lady in the movie started exclaiming, "E 'un segno, E 'un segno."

Apparently in Italy when a bird poops on your head, it's a sign. A very good sign, in fact. In America, when you crack open a bloody egg it means, well, I'm not sure what it means. But, if it's a sign, it can't be a good one.

Sadie still looked feverish, but I decided to let her go to school because I wasn't in the mood for an argument. I secretly hoped the school nurse would intervene and send her home early, but not before I got LuAnne settled in her new place. I thought about this on the drive to LuAnne's house and wondered why it was that everything hit at once. 'When it rains, it pours' was becoming a joke to me, and I was still asking why when I let myself into LuAnne's house. I called her name several times, as always, but there was no answer. Today was the biggest day; the moving men would be coming to pack up all her furniture.

Some items would be going to her suite at River Side, some would be going to our house, some would go to Goodwill for the homeless people because, according to LuAnne, homeless people need furniture. I moved from room to room calling her name, but there was still no answer. I pushed the curtains back to scan the backyard. Where could she be? The moving men would be arriving any minute, where on earth could she have gone? I stepped into the kitchen and saw a note on the table, it simply read, "I've gone to take a nap with Vernon."

Pins and needles started poking me again. Had she walked there? What if she got confused and got lost? The cemetery was a good ten miles away; she couldn't possibly walk that far. As images of her wandering around on foot crossed my mind, I looked up and, on the refrigerator, saw the flyer for Senior Transportation Services. In the next minute, I was out the door, in my car, and on the phone with Wes. Someone had to be at the house when the moving men arrived.

As I pulled into the entrance to the cemetery, I noticed a Senior Transport Services van; Lupe was behind the wheel, his full attention on his cell phone.

"Loopy." I hung my head as a part of my intelligence had just died. "Lupe."

He chuckled, "It's okay. I know you know my name."

"I'm sorry. It's just LuAnne . . ."

"I know, a week or so ago she started calling me Loopy. I really don't mind."

"Is she here? I mean, is she why you're here? Did you drive her here? I'm sorry, it's just . . ."

"Calm down, Mrs. Moore, it's okay. She's here. She called and asked if I would bring her here to see her husband. She told me I didn't need to wait, that you'd be here soon enough. But it felt wrong to leave. Until I get another

125

call I don't have anywhere to be, so I thought I'd stay as long as I could. Just to make sure she had a ride back. She seemed a little off."

"Thank you, Lupe. Really, thank you."

"No problem. I always enjoy driving her. Tell her I'll be counting the minutes till our next date." He chuckled and started the engine. I shook my head as he drove away. I was feeling more and more like I had three children instead of two. I shook my head even harder to rid myself of that thought. LuAnne wasn't a child. I wouldn't allow myself to see her that way, no matter how childlike she became.

I didn't see LuAnne right away, but if she was really napping, I wouldn't see her until I got a few rows in. And sure enough, there she was, spread out over Vernon's grave just as she had done earlier in the week. Patience had become my companion since LuAnne's diagnosis; this situation was proof of that. I wanted to scold her, but what good would it do? Her ability to make smart decisions was deteriorating along with her memory.

I walked toward her, her back to me, slowly but not softly. I wanted her to hear me coming, but I didn't want to startle her. When she didn't move, I started calling her name; repeating it until I was standing directly over her and the whole picture came into view. She lay on her side, her eyes staring straight ahead, her face white as snow. I stood staring down at her, and for a brief moment, the world went silent. I heard nothing. Nothing but the sound of struggle.

When Vernon died three years ago, Wes and I sat on either side of the bed holding his hands. LuAnne stood at the foot of the bed rubbing his feet. To anyone else, this might have seemed odd. But we knew this was a sweet—perhaps the sweetest—gesture of love. We were never certain if it was the cancer itself or the medication designed to kill the cancer, but for some reason, Vernon had muscle spasms in his feet that caused him great discomfort. LuAnne would rub them as often as he asked, whether it be with words or with the particular way his face would change when, as he would call it, the pinching started. It seemed right for her to rub his feet as he drew his last breath. It was something she could do to make him more comfortable, and she did this for several minutes after he had stopped breathing.

I've thought about that many times over the years, and I thought of it that day as I sat next to LuAnne's body waiting for Wes and the paramedics to arrive. I'm becoming, thanks to the voice inside, more and more aware of my selfishness. And I confess the selfish thought I had with LuAnne that day was that I would never rub her feet. Of course, it wouldn't have been her feet I would have rubbed, it would have been her head, as that is what brought her comfort. Once, while she was more fully herself, she told me that when I pressed my fingertips against her scalp and ran my fingers through her hair, I was helping her to forget the pain. Her pain, she had told me, was in her heart, but I couldn't very well rub that; distracting her mind was the next best thing.

Doing that, rubbing her head, playing with her hair, was how I pictured myself at LuAnne's deathbed. But now that would never happen. I wanted her to be surrounded by loved ones when she died. It broke my heart that she died alone. Although she wasn't really alone, was she? She was exactly where she wanted to be, and with the exact person she wanted to be with when she passed from this world. I couldn't help but wonder if she knew. If she sensed it coming. She seemed so unmoved by all the changes. Could she have known? This is a question Wes and I would likely mull over for the next 10,000 years. But, in the end, what did it matter? She was at rest. She boxed up her house, said her goodbyes, and went home.

I called the high school and left instructions for Sadie to walk to the elementary and wait with Finn. When she first came into view I could tell by her movements she was angry. But, because Wes and I had never picked the kids up from school together, as soon as our eyes met, her demeanor changed; she knew something was wrong.

"Did you lose your job?" Finn asked. I winked at him and shook my head no. He then leaned over to his sister and whispered, "They look lugubrious." Sadie said nothing but from the corner of my eye, I saw her gently place her hand on his knee and squeeze it softly. I had done this to Sadie and Finn a million times over the years, a means of communicating that I needed them to exist while being silent and motionless. Finn pressed Batman against his face and held him there the entire ride home. He did not move, and he did not make a sound.

We had decided beforehand that Wes would keep Finn on the front porch and talk to him there. We wiped our eyes as we imagined how the conversation would go: Finn allowing himself to cry but keeping his chin up and saying, "Good for Grandma. Now her forgetter will be fixed."

I volunteered to tell Sadie, my way of loving and protecting my husband in an already overly tense situation. Anticipating her reaction wasn't so easy. "It could go either way," Wes had said. I agreed, because grief is different for everyone, it's not a one size fits all emotion. For Sadie, it started in her hands, rubbing her wrists together so hard I feared she'd leave bruises. She then moved her right wrist to her head and started rubbing her temple; her other hand went to her belly and clutched her t-shirt. Then came the questions and accusations. "How could you let this happen? Why weren't you with her? You screw everything up; you know that? You screw up everything!"

I was tempted, for a brief moment, to defend myself. LuAnne had suffered a heart attack. How could that be my fault? But the more questions she asked, the more legitimate they sounded, and I couldn't help but think that Wes was asking himself these very same questions. I wondered if his deep sea of kindness would dry up in old age, and one day, a million years from now, he would point his finger at me in anger and say, "It could have been prevented. You should have been there. My mother's death was your fault." I wouldn't survive such an accusation—I simply wouldn't—because there would be a deeper meaning to those words. Such an accusation, such words, would penetrate each and every layer of my being and tear open wounds that still, after a lifetime, had never properly healed. Angry words were never simple, as they always found a way to connect to a memory, bringing up unrelated hurt that somehow, though worlds apart, seemed as familiar as one's own skin.

I watched Sadie, much like watching television, in the sense that I felt drawn in but also disconnected. And the weight, the almost unbearable weight of love and of love lost nestled in my chest and moved like quick growing vines through my entire body, wrapping itself around my nerve endings so that I felt nothing, heard nothing. Sadie continued to hurl questions and insults at me, but they couldn't penetrate the vines that had suddenly encased me. I couldn't tell if I was being punished or protected. But after several minutes I decided I had been protected. Her words needed to come out, but I need not carry them with me.

Finally, Sadie held up her middle finger and swung it in my direction, such an unattractive gesture for a girl. I wondered as I followed her up the stairs if she had expressed herself in that way before or had she been saving it for such an occasion as this, for me. Perhaps she'd done this to me in her mind, or had she practiced in front of her mirror? She did it with such ease; she looked so natural. So natural and unattractive.

We reached her bedroom and, at last, the words stopped, and there was only screaming. An unusual scream that sounded almost inhuman. This I could suddenly hear with a heightened sensitivity as if I were in a tunnel. While Sadie screamed, she slammed her door shut, then opened it again, then slammed it shut, then opened it again, over and over and over. I stood there, my hair blowing from the motion of her door, or maybe it was from her screams. Either way, there was something refreshing about the air rushing over me. There was also some relief in Sadie finally unleashing what had been locked inside her for far too long.

As I stood there, I thought back to that day when the letter arrived from my brother's lawyer. That evening Wes and I sat with Sadie on the front porch, for privacy but also because we thought the fresh air might make the words flow easier. Sadie promptly asked how Wes had been walking, talking, and breathing all day. Because the letter clearly stated that her dad was dead. That letter changed everything. We talked, we cried, we explained, and cried some more. And when I say "we" I mean Wes and I. Sadie sat, hearing our words, but not listening. She, in one evening, turned from our soft little girl, to a cold, stone wall. We realized it was pointless to keep explaining, to keep crying. Our words meant nothing. We could chip away at her piece by piece, but it seemed better, kinder, to leave her intact. To allow her to soften in her own time. And that's what I was seeing happen now. Not that she was softening necessarily. And not that she was suddenly letting me in. But, her screams, her outrage, told me she was finally letting it out. It, being all the rot from deep within.

I pictured Wes sitting on the front porch; his arm around Finn. I could see Finn crying and Wes running his fingers through those thick curls telling him everything would be okay. I longed to do that for Sadie. To calm her with my words and my touch. But I wouldn't do anything but stand there and let her scream until she was empty, and then I would walk away. It didn't matter how much I wanted to hold her in my arms, to wipe her tears, to reassure and comfort her. She wasn't ready. So, I would wait. I would wait until she came to me. And I was confident that she would, eventually. I was also confident that this was the hardest part of parenting. Letting your kids hurt. Knowing that sometimes the only way to soften a heart is to let it hit the floor and shatter into a million pieces.

It was Wes that came to me for comfort that night. I will always wonder if he really needed me or if he knew I needed him. I will always wonder because I will never ask and without me asking, he will never tell. Afterward, we cried and talked and cried some more. We dressed and sat on the front porch—saying nothing, yet saying everything. We went back to bed, tossing and turning until the wee hours.

As sleep finally overcame me, I found myself back in my parent's living room. My mom was crying. My dad sat staring out the window.

"Nina filed for divorce," my mom said, wiping her eyes. "The baby is due any day now, and she doesn't want her." Her shoulders shook up and down as she cried.

My dad put his arm around her and said, "Your brother doesn't want the baby either. They don't want anything that reminds them of each other."

"We'll take her," I said. "No question."

There was a noise, a creaking in the hallway that briefly brought me back to consciousness. I closed my eyes again and found myself in Cleveland on that sidewalk, my brother pushing himself against me. I could feel my body jerking as the images flashed through my mind. I couldn't take it anymore. I pulled my gun, he stepped off the curb saying the ugliest word, and out of the shadows, like a hawk snatching its prey, an SUV sped by taking his body with it.

I sat up in bed gasping for air and heard the creaking in the hallway again. Then a soft knock on our door. I turned on my lamp, and breathlessly called, "Come in."

The door opened slowly, and Sadie stood in the doorway. Sweat was dripping down her face; her cheeks were red as fire. I pushed back the covers with one hand and shook Wes with the other. Sadie stood lifeless with her arms by her sides, palms up. She muttered, "Mom" as she dropped to her knees. A moment later, she was face down on the floor.

Sometimes the most important moments in life are remembered in blurred slow motion: Wes scooping Sadie in his arms, me waking Finn, and picking him up like a toddler, his legs wrapped around my waist; getting in the car and rushing to the emergency room; all this happened in real time yet parts of the night, sure to have been important details, escaped my memory. Where was Finn when we rushed in the emergency room? When did I put my shoes on? Was Sadie conscious on the ride to the hospital? Was Finn scared, and did I comfort him? What I remember most is what happened next.

Wes was pacing the hallway, his hands on his hips. His broad shoulders slumped as they carried the weight of our world; a posture I was all too familiar with. I sat with Finn wishing I could pace with Wes, help carry the load. But this is what mothers did, they sacrificed for their children.

Finn had been doodling in a kids magazine he found on a table, but he put it down and took my hand in his; turned my arm over and rubbed my wrist with his fingers.

"Can I give you a tattoo? With my ink pen?"

"I don't know, Finn. Now doesn't seem like the time for tattoos."

"It's the perfect time," he said. "I need a distraction. And besides, it's an ink pen, not a needle. It might feel nice and relax you."

Whose kid are you? That's what I wanted to ask, but of course, I didn't.

"Sure," I told him. "Give me a tattoo."

Finn was right. It was relaxing. His ink pen slid across my skin like silk. I closed my eyes and let the sensation distract me. It might have been five minutes; it might have been an hour. I don't really know. My mind was blank. I thought of nothing. I might have questioned my own existence had it not been for the rhythmic thumping of my heart.

"Faith." Wes's voice echoed in the hallway.

"Finn, stay here." I kissed his head before walking away. I looked down briefly and noticed the dark bat symbol etched on my wrist; my face didn't change, but inside I was smiling.

"Mr. and Mrs. Moore." The doctor walked towards us with intention in his step and sadness in his eyes. I held my breath. "First let me say your daughter is going to be fine." Wes put his hand on my arm as if permitting me to exhale, but I ignored him. "Your daughter . . ." He, the doctor, put both hands in the deep pockets of his lab coat and stood up a little straighter. "Sadie has a serious infection; the result of a recent, unresolved abortion."

I audibly let out my breath, "An unresolved what?" Wes let go of my arm.

"An unresolved abortion." He put extra emphasis on the last word. "In these situations, I call them unresolved simply because they're just that. Unresolved. The procedure was not completed. Sadie needed immediate medical attention and didn't receive that attention and the result is an infection that could—"

"Wait," I said, louder than I meant to. "Wait. The procedure wasn't completed? Just wait a minute . . ." I could feel my eyes skipping around the hallway, not focusing on any one thing. I was suddenly aware of a humming sound coming from the lights. My skin felt patchy hot. For some reason, a reason I still don't understand, I licked my fingers and started rubbing off the tattoo. As I rubbed my wrist, making a thick, black, unrecognizable smear, I had an overwhelming feeling that I rarely allowed myself to feel; I desperately missed my parents.

Sadie's infection was serious. Serious enough that it might leave her sterile. A thought that infuriated and grieved me. The doctor said that ridding her body of the infection would take time. "Time would tell," he said. In time, I would wrap my head around the fact that my sixteen-year-old daughter was pregnant and that now she was not. Time would tell a lot of things. After the doctor left us, Wes needed to be alone and went to the cafeteria for coffee. This didn't bother me, that he walked away after receiving such news. I would sit with Finn and wait until we were allowed to see Sadie. I would wait to get my coffee because that's what mothers do.

A nurse moved us from the bench in the hallway to a waiting room with a television. She thought we might want to watch television as we waited to see our daughter who was recovering from an unresolved abortion. We sat, not watching television but staring at a painting on the wall opposite us. The canvas was covered in an array of messy, multicolored dots. The dots were arranged in sweeping circles all going in different directions as if a strong wind had blown in with all it's might and disrupted the order.

"What do you see?" Finn asked in a tired voice.

"What?"

"What do you see in that painting?" He pointed at the canvas, lazily lifting his arm.

What did I see? Vibrant colors that blurred together the longer I stared. The swirl of black, red, and gray reminded me of darkness, blood, and bone. I saw death.

"Mom?" Finn nudged my arm.

"The painting makes me sad," I told him.

"Really? It makes me happy."

"Does it?" I replied, not surprised that we'd see two different things.

He looked up at me; his face marked with deep lines from the creases in his pillowcase, "Remember my birthday party last year? Remember I had a piñata? Remember when I busted it open and all the candy fell out, and confetti flew everywhere? That's what the picture looks like to me, confetti!" He raised his hands in the air and wiggled his fingers.

I felt, briefly, that I might slap him. Or that I might just get up and walk out of the hospital, never looking back. But I only felt that briefly, and of course I not only stayed but spoke kindly to him. I was too tired to react to my exhaustion.

"Isn't it funny," I asked, " how we can look at the same painting and see two completely different things?"

"Perspective," he whispered.

I took a deep breath and kissed his head. "I bet you wish you had your book or something."

"I finished it," he said, yawning.

"Tell me the ending."

He rubbed his eyes, making little swishing sounds. "Arthur and Edmund were at this river bank, and they climbed up a tree for a better view, and they saw some village people on the other side, and they knew they would be rescued if they could just make it across the river. But they were still being hunted by the lion, and they knew it was waiting for them, lying in the tall, yellow grass. They couldn't see it, you know, because the lion was the same color as the grass, but they knew it was there, and they knew if they jumped down from that tree and tried to cross the river the lion would get them. So, Arthur, he's the older boy, made a plan to jump from the tree and run into the grass to distract the lion so that Edmund could get away. When Edmund figured out what Arthur was planning, he started begging him not to do it. He told him there had to be another way. But Arthur said he had figured it out. The land needed a blood sacrifice. There had to be death for there to be life. Get it? It's a metaphor; Arthur had to die so that Edmund could live. Arthur realized . . . life was in the blood. . . he realized he had to . . . make a . . . blood sacrifice."

He looked up at me with wide eyes. I started to ask more questions, but Wes came in and sat next to me, wrapping his arm around my shoulder. I leaned into him and closed my eyes. I wanted to talk more with Finn. I wanted to ask Wes if he was okay. But, I didn't do any of those things. I slipped into a deep sleep before I even realized what was happening.

When I woke, Wes's head was tilted back against the wall; he was also sleeping. I looked over to Finn, but he wasn't in his seat. I walked out in the hallway, looked in both directions, but he wasn't there. I called his name once, twice, and on the third time, Wes was by my side. He asked with his eyes where Finn was; mine answered that I didn't know.

We rushed down the hallway in different directions. I stopped at the bathroom and knocked. There was no answer. I tried to open the door, but it was locked. I knocked again.

"Finn?" This time I heard whimpering. "Finn!" I pulled on the doorknob until it finally opened. On the other side of the door stood Finn, his face covered in tears, his arms covered in blood. His entire body was trembling; I had never seen a face so full of fear.

"Wes!" I grabbed Finn and pulled him to me, "Oh, baby, what happened?"

Wes scooped Finn from my arms, and as we ran down the hallway, above Wes's cries for help, I could hear Finn choking on his tears saying, "It was for Grandma and Sadie . . . so that no more bad things will happen." Finn opened his hand and his grandfather's pocket knife, now sticky with blood, fell to the floor.

We were met by two nurses who took Finn and rushed him away from us. Wes grabbed my arm as I tried to follow. He pulled me to his chest and held me there as I wept. I couldn't take any more, I told him. I just couldn't take any more.

Wes and I were ushered into another room poorly designed for waiting where we sat in silence because, in that room, words didn't exist. Wes sat bent over with his elbows on his knees. Other than his fingers massaging his temples, he was completely still. I, on the other hand, had something in me, ants perhaps, crawling under my skin. My legs were aching, and relief only came when I bounced them. My hips were throbbing, causing me to shift in my seat every few seconds. Thin lines, like stray hairs, were tingling on my face. I bit my lips because they were numb. I frantically looked around the room as even my eyes couldn't be still, and that's when I saw him. On the end table next to me was that same magazine with my brother's picture smiling up at me, causing a hard thud in my chest. I jumped to my feet, wildly shaking my hands.

"Faith?" Wes looked at me with tired eyes.

"I can't sit here. I'm sorry. I'm going for a walk." At the door, I stopped and turned back to him, "You can come with me. I just can't sit here."

"Go ahead," he whispered.

I walked, or maybe I ran, down the hall and to the elevators. Inside I instantly felt trapped and continually pressed the ground level button. When the doors opened, I was met by a man in a wheelchair. "Oh, excuse me," he said, trying to move out of my way. Had it been possible, I would have jumped right over him, I needed out of that building, out of the chilled air and away from the smell of sterilization.

As if surfacing from a deep dive, I gasped as the night air rushed over my face. I hurried to the edge of the walkway and there, to my surprise, was our car. Not only had we not thought to come back and park it, but Wes had left the keys hanging from the ignition. I got in and started the engine. I looked up to the rows of hospital windows; somewhere in those rooms was my family. I pressed the gas pedal and sped to the exit sign and turned out onto the main road. The street lights looked like halos hanging in the air; ghostly shadows seemed to hover over the damp roads. There were two, four, then six blocks between the hospital and me. The speedometer had just reached 80 mph when I heard the voice inside ask, "Where are you going?" As my foot hit the break, skidding me to a stop, that dreaded manilla envelope slid out from under the passenger seat. I leaned over, grabbed it, and let out an accusatory, "You."

The envelope felt cold, almost damp, in my hands. My body began to shake as if I were out in the dead of winter. It felt as if someone else had taken control of the wheel as I made a u-turn and headed back to the hospital parking lot. There, under a flickering street light, I tore into the envelope and pulled out a stack of papers. There was a letter from Mr. Monroe which I moved to the bottom of the stack to read later. To my surprise what he had compiled for me was a stack of photocopied news articles; the first headline read, "Local boy molested by babysitter."

My heart hit so heavy in my chest I choked, and my face went numb. I blinked heavily as I flipped through the articles with phrases like "molested," "five years old," "caught in the act," and "tried as an adult" flashed before my eyes.

"This changes nothing," I said. Then, throwing the stack of papers back on the floorboard, I screamed it again, "This changes nothing!" I could hear myself screaming it again and again: the words, *this changes nothing*. But, of course, while I wasn't ready to admit it, this changed everything. My clenched fists banged against the steering wheel until my hands were burning and my arms began to shake from exhaustion, I climbed in the back seat and facing the rear of the car rolled as tightly as I could into a ball. I stared at the seat and thought that, with my blurry eyes, the leather resembled snakeskin; and that's when I heard it.

"You don't have to do this anymore."

The voice was so loud and so present, I startled and looked over my shoulder to see who was in the car with me. But no one was there, just me and the snakeskin. As I turned back, I noticed the seat belt in a way I had never noticed it before, and I watched my hands pull the strap and wrap it around my neck. My body fell back into the seat pulling on the strap. Within seconds my face felt fat and hot, and my eyes bulged against my eyelids. Stars appeared, flickering around my head, and I saw as if she were standing before me, my great-aunt Hazel. She was sneering at me with a cigarette lazily fixed between two fingers; with her other hand, she waved for me to follow her. As the stars became multicolored and began to flash, I felt for a moment that I was doing just that—following her. Then, as if she were whispering in my ear, I heard Sadie's soft voice, "Mom."

My eyes shot open, and air filled my burning lungs as I freed my neck from the belt. There was coughing, whimpering, then weeping. And when I could weep no more, I was overcome by sleep, and the dreaming came almost immediately. I was back in Cleveland, back on that sidewalk with my brother pressed against me. We were moving in fast motion, everything around us smeared like finger paints. Our hurried movements were brought to a halt the moment I pulled my gun and aimed at my brother. He walked towards me but something was off. Something was different, missing. He looked as though I had summoned him from the dead.

"What do you want from me?" he snapped, "An apology?"

"Permission," I whispered.

"Permission? Permission for what?"

"To write your story. Our story. All of it."

"You can't write that story," he said, inching away from me. "It was already written. You're just telling the tale." He bowed as if ending the best performance of his life and stepped off the curb. With his hollow gaze set on me, he was enveloped by an oncoming vehicle. My arm dropped to my side, my finger slid off the trigger.

Out of anger, fear, or perhaps relief, I began to cry. Next came the shaking, I tried to stand still, but I couldn't. Then I realized it wasn't just me, every car parked along the street was jerking back and forth, and then with a sudden jolt, the entire city began to shake. From above the parking garage across the street, a bright light, perhaps the brightest of lights, appeared so suddenly I had to shield my eyes and look away. But the shaking hadn't stopped and then there was a noise; what was that noise? I could hear the city vibrating, and I feared the street might open up and swallow me.

The light, no longer peeking over the garage but now showing its full self with great pride, asked me—in a language all its own—to put down my hand and behold its glory. As I lowered my hand I felt myself waking up, and as my eyes flickered open, I felt, and saw, the morning sunrise warming my face. My heart was racing, my face damp with sweat, or tears, or maybe both. I took in a deep, cleansing breath, but then realized I could still hear the city vibrating. Sitting up, I saw my cell phone sitting in the cup holder; the entire console buzzing underneath it. There were seven voicemails, all from Wes. Where was I, he wanted to know. Where had I gone? Maybe one day I would tell him I left. Tried to leave for good. But I was brought back.

Inside the hospital, a nurse escorted me to room 215. I stood in the door feeling strangely rested, a sensation I feared never feeling again. Sadie laid on her back hooked to machines and bags with fluids, a large bruise on her right cheek. Finn was cuddled up beside her, his arms wrapped in bandages. Wes was slumped in a chair next to the bed, holding Sadie's hand. All three of them asleep. I stood there, looking at my family, wondering how we got here, to this place of complete brokenness. The type of brokenness, a shattering, that so clearly required a sacrifice that even a nine-year-old could see it. As I shook my head, I realized Sadie was staring at me. She raised her free hand, and I went to her side, taking her hand and squeezing it lightly. Her fingers tightened around mine as her eyes closed again. For the first time, perhaps in my entire life, I felt gathered up rather than slipping through loose fingers. I knew then, at that moment, we'd be okay. We would heal and come back from this. Our wounds were deep; we were waterlogged with pain, but our love was deeper, and we would, in time, find higher ground.

6

Sadie would be in the hospital for almost three weeks after that day. Wes
and I would take turns staying with her, bringing Finn after school for short
visits. On one of those days, I left Sadie and Finn so they could have some
privacy. The day before, while Sadie slept, I read an article about the damaging
effects of helicopter moms. So, leaving them alone for a bit seemed like a
good idea. On that day, I walked down the hall and sat, once again, in the
poorly designed waiting room. I stared at the painting that reminded me of
death and Finn of confetti and after some time, picked up the magazine from
the chair beside me and read another article. This one was about parents
recognizing that their children will not always be children. They grow and
mature, and at some point, it's appropriate to share the things that we've
always kept from them. The secret things that we wanted to protect them
from. These secrets, apparently, have the power to take our child/parent
relationship to the next level. When we let our children know our secrets,
know who we really are, they see us as human—not just parents.

After reading this article I shared my memories with Sadie, the ones I had
written down and the ones still swimming in my head. We wouldn't hug those
memories to our chests with deep satisfaction, but we would put them in their
proper place, on the shelf in our hearts that held hurts from our pasts and
remnants of bad dreams. I also gave Sadie the envelope from the private
investigator, and let her read that in her own time. I shared with her that I had
been asked to write a biography about him, and why I had struggled so deeply
with that decision. In return, Sadie told me how finding out who her real dad
was was like finding out she had been born color blind but didn't know it, that
she had been walking around her whole life thinking the sky red when
everyone around her knew the sky was actually blue. She felt stupid, small, and

naive. She told me about the pregnancy, the abortion, and how it was her that pushed Kyle away, he hadn't left her in her moment of need. She just wanted to not need anyone. She wanted, for once, to be her own person. She admitted that hadn't turned out so well.

In this moment of transparency, I explained to her that my goal, all along, was to protect her. I didn't want to paint a terrible picture of her real dad, but there was purpose in wanting to keep it from her. I never, ever, wanted her—in her darkest moments—to think she was like him. But, in truth, she was like him. She has his smile, his love for the arts, his determination and intelligence. I had never considered that in her best moments, she might want to know where those traits came from. And, if I was being honest, that was the root of my anger. If I recognized that parts of her goodness came from him, then I had to admit there was good in him too. This truth came out of my mouth with enormous strain.

LuAnne had been in the ground for almost a month before Sadie was able to visit. We stood before the headstone, Sadie wearing her grandmother's pearls, me wearing her broach, chuckling at Finn who had written a very touching, yet very wordy, letter apologizing for not fixing her. The piece of paper was then folded, placed in a ziplock bag, and stuck on the stone with some duct tape, right below LuAnne's name. Sadie asked to be alone and sat at her grandmother's grave talking, crying, sharing what there was to be shared. Lightening her load.

It was on that day in the cemetery that I realized Sadie had her dad's strength. Both from the dad that was raising her, and the dad whose blood coursed through her veins.

"It's not your fault," Sadie said, taking my hand. "None of this is your fault."

"I wish I could believe that."

"Believe it—it's true." She squeezed my hand for an added boost of confidence. "You know, Mom, you're always saying that being normal is hard for you, but maybe normal is hard because you are normal, and being you is just hard. Like, I'm normal and being me is hard. What if we're all normal because having problems is normal? And, it's hard because life is hard, for everyone."

There are no words for the moment when you, as a parent, receive life-giving truth from your child. All I could do was stare at her, into her deep, dark eyes and marvel at the wisdom that was pent up inside them.

"My publisher called this morning," I finally said, shaking off a chill.

"What did you say?"

Again, I had no words. I just stared ahead while we stood there until the words on the headstone started to blur and Sadie squeezed my hand again.

"Mom, you should write the book. I mean, honestly . . . not to be rude, but how many people are actually going to read it?"

I let out a jolt of laughter that had been locked inside for a million lifetimes.

"Seriously, Mom. You should do it. It's just a book." And then with wide eyes, she pointed toward the headstone. There, perched on the edge, above LuAnne's name, was a hummingbird. The winged beauty then sped toward us and made a sudden stop right in front of our faces. Its wings, no more than blurs on the sides of its body, unknowingly sprayed bits of color on our world that had, for so long, been muted and grey. The bird tilted its head as if to see us better, as if to say hello, and in an instant, it was gone. I heard Sadie, and myself, let out a breath. It was then she and I both started breathing for the first time in a very long while.

That very night I started writing about my brother. I would tell the tale. The words came with such ease and clarity; I hardly skipped a beat. I would share the pieces of him that I had been carrying around, finally unpacking my load. I would gather and share stories from others who saw a different side of him. I would tell of events in his early life that had been kept from me. Events that, while they offered no excuse, offered an explanation as to what molded and shaped him. I would explain that people who have unspeakable things done to them often do unspeakable things. I would write the book, thankful that my parents weren't alive to read it. They had gone out of their way, uprooted their lives, to give my brother a fresh start—a life where no one knew what there was to know about him. But as they say, the truth will out.

I know, now more than ever, that I can take the pieces of my brother's life, as with all our lives, and scatter them on a canvas. When people stop to take notice, to really take notice, some would see a scattered mess, maybe death. But others would see a beautiful, intentional work of art. A masterpiece, perhaps confetti. I would stare at the pieces myself from time to time, the pieces of our lives, and each time I would see something new, something different, a connection I hadn't noticed before. And because we often learn about ourselves from the lives of those who came before us, I would finally unlock boxes that had been taped shut and hidden away, allowing me to see more clearly through the blurry ghosts of the past.

Now and then we, as a family, would stare at the contents of those boxes, the scattered pieces, from this angle and that, and all the while we would hear the voice inside speaking through Finn. He would be beside us whispering,

"Perspective." And perspective is exactly what I needed. I thought of LuAnne the day I submitted the final draft to my publisher, and I realized that the book itself wouldn't be, as she had said, my so much more. But through the writing of this book and the release of its hold on me, my life, my actual life, would be so much more. Maybe that's what LuAnne was trying to tell me all along. She knew, after all, what there was to know about me and that I needed, desperately, to be free of it. She also knew that, for me, freedom meant transferring the past from my heart to the page. She knew.

I love LuAnne. Then, now, and always—for this.

THE END

Beth Ann Baus

ABOUT THE AUTHOR

Beth Ann Baus has spent most of her adult life counseling women who have experienced varying degrees of abuse. It's no surprise that the horrors of abuse and the path to healing are main themes in her writing. Beth was raised in Tennessee but now makes her home in Ohio with her husband and two sons. Beth is also the author of the historical fiction novel *Sister Sunday*.

Also available at Amazon.com:

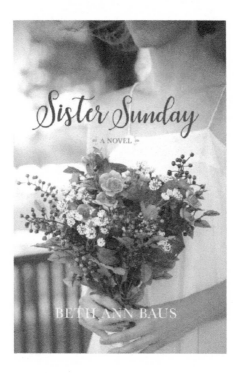

"It isn't like any other story I have read before…"

"This book wrapped me up like a warm blanket!"

"Brought me to tears."

"I couldn't put this book down!"

"Just when I thought I had their story figured out I encountered delightful twists and turns that left me glued to the pages."

"Warm & wonderful."

Made in United States
Orlando, FL
11 December 2021

11503625R00093